The Voluntary Impulse

in the same series

Wealth and Inequality in Britain
W. D. Rubinstein

The Government of Space
Alison Ravetz

Educational Opportunities and Social Change in England
Michael Sanderson

A Property-owning Democracy?
M. J. Daunton

Sport in Britain
Tony Mason

The Labour Movement in Britain
John Saville

THE VOLUNTARY IMPULSE

Philanthropy in Modern Britain

Frank Prochaska

faber and faber
LONDON · BOSTON

First published in 1988
by Faber and Faber Limited
3 Queen Square London WCIN 3AU

Photoset by Wilmaset Birkenhead Wirral
Printed in Great Britain by
Mackays of Chatham, PLC, Kent

British Library Cataloguing in Publication Data

Prochaska, Frank
The voluntary impulse: philanthropy in
modern Britain. – (Historical handbook
series).
1. Great Britain. Philanthropy
I. Title II. Series
361. 7'4'0941

ISBN 0-571-13763-6

For Alice

HISTORICAL HANDBOOKS

Series Editors:
Avner Offer – University of York
F. M. L. Thompson – Institute of Historical Research,
University of London

It is widely recognized that many of the problems of present-day society are deeply rooted in the past, but the actual lines of historical development are often known only to a few specialists, while the policy-makers and analysts themselves frequently rely on a simplified, dramatized, and misleading version of history. Just as the urban landscape of today was largely built in a world that is no longer familiar, so the policy landscape is shaped by attitudes and institutions formed under very different conditions in the past. This series of specially commissioned handbooks aims to provide short, up-to-date studies in the evolution of current problems, not in the form of narratives but as critical accounts of the ways in which the present is formed by the past, and of the roots of present discontents. Designed for those with little time for extensive reading in the specialized literature, the books contain bibliographies for further study. The authors aim to be as accurate and comprehensive as possible, but not anodyne; their arguments, forcefully expressed, make the historical experience available in challenging form, but do not presume to offer ready-made solutions.

Contents

	Preface	xiii
I	Introduction	1
II	Philanthropy ascendant	21
III	Parochial service in practice	41
IV	Paying the bills	59
V	Challenges and adaptation	69
VI	Conclusion	86
	Notes	91
	Bibliography	97
	Index	103

Preface

Modern British philanthropy is a vast and important subject, but one which has not aroused a great deal of historical scholarship, despite the richness of the sources. Compared to the writings on the Welfare State, there is relatively little to work from, though in recent years this has begun to change, a trend which is likely to continue with the resurgence of interest in contemporary charity. Charting philanthropy's evolution is a complicated business because of its many byways and cul-de-sacs, and because it has been so bound up with the evolution of the Welfare State in the historiography. The tendency to see it as a stage in the development of the statutory social services has not been helpful to our appreciation of its persistence and variety. The provision of welfare is central to philanthropy, but it is far from being its sole concern. Nor should we forget that much benevolence takes place in areas which fit ill with a view to welfare inherited from the state. For their part, Victorian philanthropists commonly held a holistic view to human life. They did not usually make distinctions, which to them were arbitrary, between religious and social welfare. In a time when medicine could do so much less for the body, the needs of the soul demanded more attention. Institutions whose objects were educational or recreational had underlying moral, if not spiritual, purposes and were part of a pattern of benevolence often seen as having a welfare element.

Like many others, historians of social policy are often alienated by the now unfashionable pieties and hierarchical values associated with nineteenth-century charity. Whether collectivist or not, they habitually study those trends which illuminate present issues as defined by the state, a tendency reinforced by the accessibility of government records as opposed to charitable ones. There are books on Victorian England which treat the subject of social reform without any reference to philanthropy at all, a feat which would leave Victorians quite dumbfounded. The phrase 'from charity to social work', the title of a book on welfare reform, suggests the way in which philanthropy is more commonly treated. It is of interest essentially because it anticipates or encourages state action.

Given the Whiggishness, or teleology, which runs through much of the historiography, important issues in the history of philanthropy have been ignored. The charity of the poor to the poor has hardly been touched, for it fits uncomfortably with the conception of philanthropy as middle class and patronizing. The traditions of parochial service and local charity, so crucial to understanding the Victorian way of life, have fared little better. Nor have female philanthropists been well served by the emphasis on the relationship between philanthropic bodies and the state. Largely excluded from political life until this century, women voluntarists appear infrequently in government records; and with lives typically centred on home and parish, they have not attracted much attention from historians interested in prominent charities, state welfare departments and national policy. In short, the shifting relationship between private and state responsibility for poor relief is an important and inviting issue, but a preoccupation with it distorts our appreciation of the role of philanthropy, past and present.

In a book of this size, it is impossible to do justice to more than a few of the millions of British charitable institutions active in the past two centuries. I confess that the commonplace has interested me rather more than the exceptional, and thus I have consciously given much of my attention to local institutions and humble labours which I believe typify British philanthropy. Nor have I dwelled on those dominant personalities, such as Florence Nightingale and Lord Nuffield, whose important work has been celebrated elsewhere, for my interest is rather to emphasize the social role of charity in the daily lives of ordinary people and to provide an interpretation largely grounded in their experience. Should a few of today's estimated seven million philanthropists, whether they work formally in societies or informally in their homes and neighbourhoods, come away from this book with a deeper understanding of charitable traditions and their place in them, it will have served its purpose. I hope that some historians and others outside the voluntary world also will find it of interest.

I would like to thank the editors of *Historical Handbooks*, Michael Thompson and Avner Offer, for the opportunity to write this book and for their encouragement and advice. George Behlmer, John Campbell, John Dinwiddy, John Eyler and Geoffrey Finlayson have given me assistance on detailed points. I am also indebted to various institutions, including the National Council for Voluntary Organisations, the King Edward's Hospital Fund for London, the Wellcome Institute for the History of Medicine, the British Library, the Greater London Record Office, and the Institute of Historical Research, University of London. My greatest debt is, as ever, to my wife and fellow historian, Alice Prochaska, who read the manuscript with a liberal and kindly eye.

Frank Prochaska
London

I

Introduction

Voluntary traditions have been overshadowed by state provision in the public mind since the Second World War. Against the background of a mass electorate, wartime distress, and the growing emphasis on material life, welfare issues shot upwards on the agenda of central government. As social policy became increasingly nationalized, charitable institutions, typically local and autonomous, were no longer newsworthy. The creation of the National Health Service pushed the voluntary sector to the periphery of the debate on health. Associated welfare legislation pushed it to the periphery of the debate on social security. To socialist critics charities were the residue of a discredited Victorian liberalism soon to be swept aside by the all-conquering state. Transfixed by the Welfare State and its role in their election prospects, politicians of varying hues narrowed discussions of social policy to government action. In the altered circumstances, social commentators sympathetic to the voluntary sector relegated it to the role of government helpmeet, or in the parlance of the 1960s the 'junior partner in the welfare firm'.[1] The more philanthropy was seen narrowly in its welfare role and studied in relation to government, the more marginal it came to be seen by those predisposed to state solutions. The tendency of welfare departments in local and central government to dismiss differing perceptions of social need added to the general disregard of voluntary activities.[2]

But the decline of philanthropy has been exaggerated. With collectivism in retreat and the growing uncertainty surrounding welfare provision, this fact is beginning to sink in. Though little reported, voluntary traditions carried on with considerable vigour after 1945, shifting ground where necessary and pioneering terrain which the state dared not enter. Moreover, a concentration of attention on those charities fulfilling welfare services obscured the many other voluntary campaigns which prospered. When charities did decline, it often had more to do with improved living standards or advances in medicine and technology than with the pattern of relations with state departments. The expansion of statutory services after the war had erratic effects on voluntary bodies. Some charities were left without a function and disappeared. Others revised their objects. Many remained unchanged. And others still started up because of post-war shortages and aspirations. MIND (1946), War on Want (1951), the Samaritans (1953) and Help the Aged (1963) are just a few prominent examples. The effects of expanding state services on kindly relatives, friends and neighbours were likewise erratic. But more of them also carried on as before than might be imagined.

The drift of opinion away from statutory welfare provision in recent years has now begun to broaden the public's awareness of the range of philanthropic activity. Though it has not often reached the headlines since the war, voluntarism shows signs of coming back into prominence. If the publicity surrounding the concerts and telethons for Ethiopian famine relief is any guide, it is coming back into fashion. As the Marxist historian Eric Hobsbawm remarked in a recent issue of the *New Statesman*, world hunger and social crisis suggested socialist remedies in the 1930s. 'Today it suggests to most people that they should give more to Oxfam or Band Aid.'[3] Innovation and cost effectiveness are thought to be among the principal virtues of contemporary philanthropy, and these have become increasingly apparent against the background of government economies and the spiralling costs and bureaucratic inefficiencies of the state welfare services. No less important are the virtues of democratic pluralism inherent in voluntary action, which are being more widely recognized by political economists of various persuasions. Thus voluntarism has broad, if muted, political support today, from left-wing socialists committed to politically-charged community action groups to right-wing conservatives who see a larger role for volunteers in a privatized health service. Just what such a privatization scheme would mean for voluntarism is unclear, but like other politically contentious issues, it is one that many charitable officials wish to avoid.[4]

Whatever the merits of specific proposals, many social commentators have concluded that in welfare, as in other spheres, small is beautiful. If social engineering was the fashion in post-war Britain, welfare pluralism, with its emphasis on democratic local initiative, is increasingly the language of the 1980s. Galvanized by the crisis in the Labour Party, some on the left have gone so far as to reject the equation of socialism with collectivism and now favour decentralized charities and cooperatives in the tradition of 'libertarian socialism'.[5] A leading advocate of voluntarism argues: 'when the conventional options of left and right are locked in the "welfare stalemate", when the *status quo* faces an increasing barrage of criticism, and when rapid social and economic change cries out for adaptability, what might be called "*gradualist welfare pluralism*" does at least offer a way forward.'[6] With its emphasis on local decision-making, innovation and self-help, a flourishing voluntary sector would, in this view, constructively intervene between large state institutions and the individual. Government, apart from its responsibility for providing those essential services associated with a modern welfare state, would allocate funds, promote policies and pass legislation which fostered and protected voluntary initiatives. In doing so they would further integrate statutory and community services, diversify the provision of welfare and, by implication, promote democracy and individual accountability.

The rising revenues of voluntary societies and the growing use of their services by the government are clear signs that welfare pluralism is increasingly attractive. Of course, in so far as government reduces funds for welfare provision or makes it more difficult to collect benefits, the demand for charitable resources is likely to increase. Some have argued that the poor now find it easier and more agreeable to use charitable agencies than to collect state benefits. In what amounts to a tacit acceptance that voluntary bodies are a very effective way to deliver a range of personal social services, the state has offered voluntary groups a more prominent role in their planning and provision, though in practice this has not gone far enough to satisfy committed voluntarists. The establishment of the Voluntary Services Unit in 1972, now in the Home Office, was an indication of government's greater respect for voluntary effort. In its various guises government has also increased its payments to charities in the last decade to an extent that it is now the largest single contributor to philanthropic causes. In 1976, government sources contributed £175 million of that year's £3,000 million or so in charitable revenue through grants and fees. In 1984, philanthropic revenues had risen to an estimated £10,000 million; government funding had risen to about £1,000 million or ten per cent of this figure.[7] Of this public money about 70 per cent is today given to welfare causes, ranging from local authority contributions to care groups to large DHSS grants to great medical charities. The state further subsidizes institutions registered by the Charity Commissioners with a range of fiscal benefits. The 1986 budget, with its American-style 'tax bonanza' for charities, is further evidence that the government looks on voluntarism with benevolence.

The growth of voluntary provision is not without its dangers, as voluntarists are aware. They are, for example, under increasing pressure to provide a greater measure of goods and services in support of the Health Service. But most of them would prefer to avoid responsibilities which they have come to see as properly those of government and which distract them from their important role in the development of new ideas and projects. Above all, there is the fundamental issue of finance. Voluntarists find it difficult to resist the temptation to accept public funds, but they worry that a growing dependence on the state will undermine their independence. In some quarters there is an underlying fear that government penetration of voluntary bodies is a threat to democracy. All too often voluntarists are caught in a crossfire between their paymasters and their communities. Such problems are also found in the United States, where it has been estimated that US federal programmes contribute about half of all the financial assistance to non-profit social services and community organizations. But the evidence thus far is that this high level of funding has not undermined the autonomy of American charities because of the low level of accountability demanded by government.[8] The same may not be true of Britain, despite its lower level of overall public funding. Seen against the background of the Welfare State, British voluntarism has an ambiguity about it which is not the case in the United States. British charities often revolve around community *needs*, and many people assume that ultimately government must take responsibility for such matters.

But where do British voluntary bodies draw the line on government financial assistance? With increasing demands on scarce resources, a theme which runs through the history of philanthropy, they urgently need financial support; yet their activities are likely to be unsettled and constrained by the vagaries of the prevailing political priorities. This is particularly noticeable in their dealings with local authorities, where some voluntary groups have become politicized. Here the situation can change overnight because of a by-election or a central government decision, which leads to a reduction in local government spending or stop-go policies. Government rate-capping and the abolition of the Greater London Council created havoc among voluntary bodies. The withdrawal of government funding following the abolition of the metropolitan counties reduced the revenues of voluntary groups in Merseyside by almost half.[9] Among those hardest hit were projects dealing with unemployment and equal opportunities. The difficulties are likely to increase given the Conservative government's centralizing tendencies and its hostility to many local government policies. If the trend toward reducing local government expenditure continues, the role of the voluntary sector in defending participatory pluralism and the democratic rights of minorities and other vulnerable groups will not be unaffected.

Aware of the danger that he who pays the piper calls the tune, the National Council for Voluntary Organisations, the leading umbrella group for voluntary bodies in Britain, has published a code for those societies in receipt of government funds. It advises them against becoming too dependent on state aid, especially if it means compromising aims and objectives. The dangers are particularly marked in those organizations which sign contracts with government authorities to provide a specific service, such as youth training or citizens' advice. In such cases they are often led into a political quagmire and find themselves at odds with their paymasters. The experience of those voluntary bodies working with the Manpower Services Commission on training and job-creation schemes is a case in point. Programme changes and sudden cutbacks in their funding in 1984 created confusion and some bitterness, as voluntarists discovered that their aims were not in line with government thinking. Difficulties continued with the Youth Training Scheme (YTS), which found little room for charitable agencies. The irony is that in the 1970s philanthropists were the pioneers of such programmes. To the voluntary sector the moral is clear: government is a volatile partner. It is happy to work with voluntarists when convenient, but it is not always reliable as shifts in political fortune and fluctuations in the economy dictate changes of policy. Victorian philanthropists, who pioneered the pattern of relations between public and private bodies, would recognize the problem. But, as we shall see, they were more confident that they retained their independence and predominance even when they went cap in hand to government. On occasion, they severed relations with the state and made do without its money.

The latter-day degree of reliance on government has barely dimmed British voluntary traditions. As in the past, when an individual has an enthusiasm, he or she buys a notebook, 'prints "minute book" carefully on the first page, calls together some . . . friends under the name of a Committee – and behold a new voluntary society is launched'.[10] This impulse to organize oneself and one's neighbours in a cause is one of Britain's most distinctive traditions. Before this century it was thought to be the most beneficial and wholesome way of promoting social harmony and individual well-being. Even in an age of vastly increased state welfare services, voluntarists have shown themselves to be remarkably resilient. From informal helpers dropping in on a neighbour, to paid officials in established societies, they display a capacity for innovation, self-sacrifice, and self-help which are traditional hallmarks of philanthropic effort. Uncommercial, they are free to concentrate their energies uninhibited by the profit motive. Individualistic, they provide a democratic safeguard, rescuing the citizen from the state's standardizing process. While their activities often receive state assistance and not infrequently pave the way for government intervention, they are tenaciously independent. The voluntary impulse may be seen as the antithesis of collective or statutory authority.[11]

It is impossible to give a precise, all-embracing definition of voluntarism; it has to do with the question of independence rather than the kind of activity pursued. For the purposes of this book, it has been restricted to what traditionally would be deemed philanthropic or charitable, or which today is sometimes called 'voluntary social action'. (Voluntary institutions such as trade unions and friendly societies often have a charitable dimension, but tthey have been excluded here in the interests of managing the subject.) Ideological challenges to collectivism, combined with constraints in public expenditure, have contributed to the revival of interest in voluntarism. But this revival cannot be explained simply by reference to cuts in statutory services, disenchantment with state bureaucracy or the Conservative government's fiscal encouragement to the voluntary sector. The philanthropic heart beats persistently, if erratically, in Britain. In a time when the public has ever-greater expectations of personal and social life, which no government, however benevolent, could satisfy, increasing numbers of people have joined together in schemes for social improvement. Whether they call their work voluntarism, community action, or the traditional usage of philanthropy or charity, the possibilities in self-help and helping others are intoned today in a manner reminiscent of a hundred years ago.

Philanthropy is defined as love of one's fellow man, an action or inclination which promotes the well-being of others. It is usually studied from the point of view of institutions, but as it implies a personal relationship it is useful to think of philanthropy broadly as kindness. This opens up the subject to include casual benevolence within the family or around the neighbourhood, activities which often expand and lead to the creation of formal societies. It also helps us to avoid the misconceptions inherent in assuming that charity is invariably a relationship between rich and poor, particularly the view, still current among social historians, that through philanthropic agencies the wealthy simply foster a subservient class of Mr Pooters. Helping others informally is a deeply-rooted tradition in Britain, as elsewhere. A necessity in working-class communities, it is widespread among all social classes. It often springs from little more than an impulse, triggered by the needs and aspirations of people who see themselves as part of a community, whether it be the family, the neighbourhood or the nation at large.

The level of casual benevolence will, of course, vary with the needs and character of a community, with the seasons and the trade cycle. Expressed in myriad ways, it remains a powerful, though little appreciated, force for social stability. Reports of a disintegration of British family life have been in the news for over a century, but we should not assume that this reflects a marked deterioration in familial kindness or community care. Attempts to measure the extent of informal philanthropy have not provided much precise information. And in a society obsessed with statistical precision this may account for its being largely ignored or taken for granted. (If it could be costed in terms of savings to the Exchequer, perhaps it would be more highly valued.) 'The extent of neighbourliness, especially in times of adversity, cannot be overstressed,' remarked a student of one working-class district of Liverpool in the 1950s.[12] More recent investigations have confirmed this opinion. In Bradford, for example, for every voluntary worker in the social service agencies there were four others providing informal, but regular, neighbourly help.[13] The Nathan Committee, which investigated various charitable practices in the 1950s, uncovered a rich seam of unpublicized neighbourliness and familial kindness; it concluded that such actions made 'satisfactory social relationships possible'.[14] Though social mobility and the larger number of women at work pose threats to these traditions, they remain an enduring strength of the nation's social life. Governments, or charities for that matter, which undermine informal benevolence do so at a cost.

Formal charitable societies draw on the traditions of informal benevolence and have usually sought to work through families and communities to combat specific distresses. Charities typically get their start in the particularity of familial or local need, a characteristic which applies to communities whatever their social make-up. (Today, locally organized neighbourhood schemes such as pensioners' clubs and playgroups are, if anything, more numerous in working-class areas than elsewhere.)[15] The diversity of family experience and local opinion creates the specialized character of much philanthropic activity. In the nineteenth century various afflictions, many of them now largely forgotten, resulted in the formation of numerous charities geared to the immediate needs of the community. Truss societies, for example, were prominent in port towns and manufacturing districts, where an estimated 20 per cent of the male population suffered from hernias.[16] Parochial charities, such as district visiting societies and mothers' meetings, dealt with a host of issues at the local level, from feeding infants to supporting the aged poor. With an intimate knowledge of the neighbourhood, they were well placed to cope quickly and effectively with many individual cases. The ability of charitable societies to respond to local challenges and initiatives and to draw on traditions of informal benevolence are among philanthropy's abiding strengths.

The continuity of charitable traditions, especially at the local level, is a major theme of this book. Preoccupied by government intervention, war and social change, historians and social commentators have largely ignored the persistence of philanthropy. Moreover, the pieties and social assumptions of Victorian charity have made it a subject which causes embarrassment in some circles, even among voluntarists. Sensitive to image and language they are, naturally enough, anxious to portray themselves and their causes as up to date. Consequently, historical associations sometimes appear a burden. As a recent publication on voluntarism stated: 'The traditions of 19th century do-gooding continue to colour the public image of the voluntary sector'.[17] Presumably, this is an oblique criticism of the influence of women on Victorian charity. But does a denigration of the nation's philanthropic past serve the interests of contemporary charities, many of them long established and dependent on the work of women? Causes may come and go with the seasons or the trade cycle, but contemporary approaches to those perennial problems such as disease, child abuse and immorality have been shaped by long experience. So too have methods of organization and fund-raising. A finer appreciation of former charitable practice has its uses, not least in giving contemporary societies that measure of respectability which comes from being part of a rich, libertarian tradition.

The dimensions and resources of contemporary philanthropy show just how vital this tradition is. Though it is an incomplete guide to institutions which have a philanthropic function, there are over 160,000 charities currently registered with the Charity Commissioners in Britain. This figure constitutes about 40 per cent of the nation's more than 350,000 voluntary organizations, which includes such diverse bodies as churches, sports clubs and trade unions. Many of the registered charities are parish-based and have only small sums to distribute; only about 50,000 have annual incomes in excess of £1,000, and probably fewer than 5,000 have incomes in excess of £10,000 per annum.[18] As the financial statistics for charities are unstandardized and only patchily available, they must be treated with caution. But much of the total charitable income of today's registered charities, put at over £10,000 million a year, is accounted for by large institutions with their many branches raising funds locally, which are concerned with education, health, and overseas aid.[19]

In terms of manpower, there were over 200,000 paid employees in the charitable sector by 1980. A difficulty arises in assessing the hours expended by unpaid volunteers because many societies do not keep such records. But it has been estimated that around 7 million volunteers, or almost 20 per cent of the adult population, participated directly, albeit most of them part time, in the provision of charitable services.[20] (Such figures encourage many politicians to promote voluntary work as a solution to youth unemployment. In the nineteenth century it served as a principal occupation for bored middle-class women, whose idleness was enforced by custom.) By 1980, the labour expended by both paid and unpaid workers was calculated to be the equivalent of about 2.5 per cent of the total labour force. If we added the many other voluntary organizations with a popularly accepted charitable function but without charitable status, the figures would be greater. How much greater still would they be should the unrecorded kindness of family and neighbours be fully assessed? It has been estimated that there are over a million 'carers' in the community who, at considerable sacrifice to themselves, look after aged or disabled relatives with little, if any, assistance from the state or charitable organizations.[21]

The thousands of new charities registered by the Charity Commissioners each year (just under 4,000 in 1986 alone), are evidence of philanthropy's vitality and its capacity to respond to changing social needs and expectations.[22] Yet the sectarian and personal nature of much charitable endeavour, combined with the legacy of the past, means that the allocation of charitable resources does not bear a direct relationship to today's social priorities, in so far as they are agreed. Moreover, it often leads to a duplication of effort and an overlapping of charitable authority. This was, of course, also true in the nineteenth century, and it resulted in much criticism of charitable uses and abuses. Criticism of charitable duplication remains today and often derives from those with a model of administration drawn from government, where overlapping responsibilities are much disliked. But is it appropriate to subject philanthropists to the planning restrictions which are applied to statutory authorities? As one student of social policy has remarked, 'In the voluntary sector . . . duplication can serve a useful function as a source of change as well as of choice and variety'.[23]

When the Wolfenden committee looked into charitable practices in the 1970s, it noted that residents in old county towns were served better by charitable bodies than the poor in industrial cities. Such disparities have led some reformers to conclude that competing institutions should amalgamate or rethink their allocations and that the definition of charity in law should be broadened to include many voluntary bodies which fall outside the present guidelines for charitable registration. But in a democratic society splintered by class, regional and doctrinal allegiances, in which the needs of the giver as well as the recipient are important, the distribution of charitable resources is bound to be at variance with any centrally agreed priorities. Accountability for malpractice is a priority, and one which the Charity Commission needs sufficient funds to enforce. But a degree of muddle and confusion must be expected and tolerated in a society in which people bridle at being told how to spend their money or to utilize their spare time. Ultimately, voluntary bodies are susceptible to market forces, at least those operating out of annual income; and consumers, who have the freedom to choose between competing institutions, will largely determine the success or failure of a given charity.

Though not without their critics, voluntarists respond in their various ways to virtually every human need and aspiration, much of it, as in the past, unsung labour carried out at home or around the neighbourhood. Among today's formal societies, many are in the medical field. Every illness and disability finds support, from spina bifida to senile dementia (two competing cancer research funds currently top the money list). Charities associated with particular trades and professions often date to the nineteenth century and assist, among others, necessitous actors, advertisers, solicitors, and pawnbrokers. Those which serve the clergy tend to be older.[24] Though less prominent today, religious charities such as the Bible Society (1804), and the London City Mission (1835) remain active. Women's organizations, from the Mothers' Union (1876) to local homes for battered wives, carry on the rich tradition of female philanthropy. Children are served by a host of institutions. Many of them, like the National Society for the Prevention of Cruelty to Children (1884), date to the late nineteenth century when the issue of child welfare came increasingly to the fore. Virtually every species of animal in the kingdom, from whales to moles, is provided for. The World Wildlife Fund (1961) looks after the interests of selected animals abroad. The Anti-Slavery Society (1823) and Oxfam (1942) are among those which look after the interests of selected foreigners. Nor are inanimate objects neglected which affect the quality of life, from footpaths to country houses. The National Trust (1895), with an income of over £70 million in 1985, is one of the most lavishly funded societies in the country. Among the charities coming into greater prominence in recent years are playgroups, societies in aid of single parents and AIDS-related institutions. Many others, including some with political overtones, are knocking on the doors of the Charity Commissioners.

The well-informed would recognize most of the national societies cited here, but on the ground in the localities these institutions are not that visible, though many of them have shops in the high street. It is important to emphasize that charitable activity largely takes place locally, in small autonomous groups or in branches of national charities. As recent studies have pointed out, most voluntary organizations have a nucleus of about twenty active members.[25] As mentioned, they often begin with an individual or family with a problem who join together with others having similar difficulties. The Samaritans resulted from the chance remark of a coroner to the Revd Chad Varah, that a girl might not have committed suicide had someone taken the trouble to talk to her.[26] Characteristically, charities come into existence through a magazine article or a notice in the local papers. Others are church-sponsored organizations, dealing with parochial needs. Many are the result of initiatives from officials of the local authorities, who see a particular problem that is best tackled by volunteers. Those set up to assist national charities either emerge because of local initiative or are inaugurated by the national organization itself as part of its development programme. Whatever their origins, these local branches are primarily concerned with fund-raising, the provision of a local service, or both. The Royal National Lifeboat Institution (1824) is not unusual in having some 2,000 fund-gathering branches across Britain.

The philanthropic world has always had an insatiable appetite for money; and while it increasingly accepts government funds, it continues to make its essential appeal to the public directly. Innovation has been the hallmark of fund-raising and today's campaigns use the latest in technology and show business to extract the proverbial widow's mite. The business community, itself a growing source of charitable revenue, offers consultancy at low cost, and advertising agencies mastermind the product line of leading charities. Direct mail, radio and television carry the message of compassion to many members of the public outside the normal fund-raising channels. Charities are continually proposing new methods of using the media, including videos and advertising more widely on radio and television with the growing deregulation of broadcasting. (There is a direct line between the lantern lectures of Victorian charities, the films used to raise funds for the voluntary hospitals in the inter-war years and the latest promotional video.) Despite the dangers of what the Americans call compassion fatigue, charities pull few punches today. The hard sell is delivered by dramatic ads of starving families in Africa or battered babies in Britain. The soft sell remains as intensive as ever, with the use of subtle pressures, to promote fund-raising drives. A charity inactive in raising money may be seen to have run out of ideas.

According to one cynic, a philanthropist is a person who can make you grin while picking your pocket; and today every effort is made to provide a laugh or a distraction. Among the latest innovations is the charity fast, which presumably carries on from the charity dinner. Despite complaints, raffles and gambling on the football pools have proved highly rewarding to many charities. Variants on shopping, long associated with charitable fund-raising, have been even more profitable. Charity organizers soon discovered that few things motivate a philanthropist more than picking up a bargain or winning a prize while performing a duty. Thus bazaars and church fêtes carry on much as they did in the nineteenth century. So do charity shops, which are not an invention of Oxfam but have their origins in the 1820s. Rock concerts, charity walks, runs and races (the 1988 London Marathon raised an estimated £9 million) extend a long tradition which began with the charity balls, concerts and cruises. The Live Aid concerts, watched by 1.5 billion people worldwide, many of whom probably could not find Ethopia on a map, raised so much money in Britain that domestic voluntary groups feared that their revenues would plummet. (They did not, in part because much of the money came from people new to charitable giving.) In some respects it evoked in the British audience attitudes to Africa reminiscent of subscribers to nineteenth-century missionary societies. In the publicity surrounding it, it was an event reminiscent of the great Anti-Corn Law League Bazaar of 1845 in Covent Garden Theatre, which raised an enormous sum while politicizing the middle classes.

Community events such as country fêtes and urban carnivals are particularly revealing of many of voluntarism's enduring themes. The annual Fulham Carnival may be seen as typical of countless charitable festivals in aid of local causes. The one held in Bishops Park in May 1987 was an unsung example of a working partnership between volunteers and a local authority. As in nineteenth-century fêtes and bazaars, there was little indication of class tension or any overt social subordination of the poor, rather an expression of cooperative benevolence and the happy intermingling of professional people with Fulham's traditional working-class inhabitants. As with most charitable functions, the occasion provided a ready outlet for individual expression. The mother with her infant 'born in the West London' holding a nappy opened for contributions to the Hospital caught the eye. Whether participating in or simply watching the street procession, children had an outing; local businesses and the police had an opportunity for publicity and improved public relations; and politicians, with an eye on the general election, had an ideal backdrop for discreet campaigning. For most participants, however, the occasion was simply a day out, perhaps a good time, an expression of pride in Fulham. In the peculiar mix of commerce and amusement, the act of charity seemed natural and diverting, a part of day-to-day life.

Most large charities blend nationally organized events with fund-raising at the familial or local level, usually through those auxiliaries established for soliciting patronage. Action Aid (1972), one society which reaches into the community through coffee mornings and school fairs, remarked in a recent report that 'thousands of small events made the difference in raising funds'.[27] Despite the traditional dependence of charities on small-scale community contributions, however, large public events and glossy advertising have become increasingly prominent in the fiercely competitive world of voluntary societies. But they can be a costly, artificial business requiring huge outlays of capital which many voluntary groups can ill afford. (Fourteen charities already spend over £1 million a year on fund-raising.) The public, which often takes expert advice before parting with hard-earned funds, might conclude that a society is profligate which can afford high-profile advertising and 'personalized' begging letters.

A reputation for good housekeeping is essential if voluntary institutions hope to continue to receive public support. Reports in the press of charitable malpractice tend to erode public confidence. An all-party group of MPs recently discovered that large numbers of charities had administrative costs amounting to more than 60 per cent of income. The great majority had not even submitted annual accounts to the Charity Commissioners, which is required by statute, in the past five years.[28] Well-run charities expect to keep their administrative and fund-raising costs below 15 per cent of income, though the target figure varies from society to society, depending on its function. Charity accountants can be highly creative and their figures for administrative costs must be taken with a grain of salt. Having said that, recent figures for Britain's twenty-one leading charities show that for every pound donated less than 10 pence went on overheads.[29] This represents a level of 'profit' unknown to commercial companies, with their better-paid managers and more heavily unionized staff. Among the most cost-effective charities were Band Aid (1986), Cancer Research Campaign (1923), Dr Barnardo's (1866) and Save the Children (1919).

Thriving on advertisement, charities merge philanthropy and fashion. As in the nineteenth century, every effort is made to get favourable notices and glamorous backers, preferably with a title. The Royal family is not large enough to serve the needs of 160,000 charities, though the Queen alone lends her name to 2,000 of them. Fresh faces like Prince Edward and the Duchess of York are much in demand and have shown promise as patrons. The charities they support will undoubtedly improve their finances. Save the Children has seen its income rise dramatically since the Princess Royal gave it her enthusiastic backing. Prince Edward focused attention on several select charities, and himself, through the 'Royal Knockout', a television event which well illustrates the perennial search for new gimmicks and entertainments to promote philanthropic causes. Failing a Royal, celebrities and public figures will do; smaller charities employ lesser lights, perhaps a magistrate or a local worthy. Village fêtes exploit vicars and their wives as relentlessly as ever. Such pillars of the establishment are not always wanted, of course. In the many soup kitchens run during the miners' strike in 1984–5, for example, the presence of Dennis Skinner or Arthur Scargill was more in keeping. The advantages of such attachments are reciprocal, for it gives respectability and opportunities for display to both patrons and charities. Celebrity status, knighthoods, and not a few votes have been given to those seen to be charitable patrons.

The need for a public image of cost-efficiency and glamour is all the more urgent since the introduction of the 'payroll-giving' scheme in 1987, which brings charities into partnership with those British companies willing to participate. The idea is not altogether new. Dr Barnardo's, for one, has had donations straight from wage packets since early this century, and already brings in about £2 million a year in this way. (In America, payroll schemes contribute $3 billion to charities.)[30] But British charities, and many British industries too it appears, are enthusiastic about the potential of an innovation which allows company employees tax relief on donations of up to £240 a year to a cause or causes of their choice. Though a ceiling of £240 is thought too modest by most voluntarists, it is estimated that if only one employee in ten contributes this sum it would generate about £400 million in additional charitable revenue each year. Early indications are that 'give as you earn' has not lived up to the expectations of its promoters. Only time will tell whether this 'new' charitable revenue reduces government payments to voluntary bodies.

Large, well-established societies with charitable status and effective lobbyists are likely to be the principal beneficiaries of the recent payroll scheme. Voluntary societies which have been refused charitable status, often small local agencies, will have to look elsewhere for funds unless the law of charity is reformed in their favour. The payroll scheme, along with other changes relating to charities in recent Conservative budgets, has made the advantages of charitable registration increasingly apparent. Apart from the respectability which it confers, itself no small matter in fund-raising, are important exemptions from most forms of direct taxation, on the condition that a charity's funds are 'applied' charitably. Among the other financial incentives are a reduction on the amount of stamp duty paid on conveyances and relief from rates paid to local authorities for premises occupied for charitable purposes. Recent budgets have also extended VAT relief to a range of new areas. All in all, the advantages of charitable status, worth over £2,500 million a year to registered institutions, far outweigh any disadvantages of coming under the authority of the Charity Commissioners and the scrutiny of the Charities Division of the Inland Revenue. The longstanding campaign to widen the range of objects which qualify for charitable status is a reflection of this fact.

The Charity Commission, set up in 1853 to remedy the misapplication of endowed charities, has had, since 1960, the additional responsibility of regulating 'collecting' charities, whose incomes derive from subscriptions and grants rather than endowments. With a small staff it has been cautious in widening the rather arbitrary definition of charity which it inherits from the courts. Many voluntarists have been alarmed to discover upon applying for charitable status that in the eyes of the law their activities are not deemed charitable. But why are the British Goat Society and Eton College registered charities, they ask, while other organizations are not which qualify as charitable in the popular meaning of the word? Though relatively few voluntary organizations have political objectives, the degree to which politics and charity can be reconciled is a contentious issue. Under existing law a political purpose is incompatible with charitable status, though the question as to whether ancillary political activity is permissible is less clear. Should an institution such as the Lord's Day Observance Society (1831) now come up for registration its charitable status would be uncertain because of its policy of bringing pressure to bear on government to promote its aims. As the Charity Commissioners admit, 'Charity law is not always governed by logic, nor are the decisions entirely consistent'.[31]

Voluntarists have been quick to put forward their views on what needs to be done in a time when boundaries between voluntary and statutory provision are unclear and open to adjustment. Indeed, their innovation here is in keeping with their innovation elsewhere. For a start, many of them want a wholesale redefinition of charitable purpose in law which would widen the range of charitable objects to include contemporary concerns such as human rights and job creation. A relaxation of the bar on the political activities of charities would thus seem to be necessary. The Charity Commission has been much criticized of late for inefficiency and for a failure to address abuses more vigorously.[32] Its many supporters in the voluntary world, worried that charitable malpractice threatens their good names, would like to see it reformed and upgraded and given sufficient resources to fulfil its duty under the 1960 Act. It is ironic that in a time of government enthusiasm for voluntarism, the Charity Commission has had to struggle against Treasury cuts. With a larger and more dynamic administration, it could bring the register up to date through computerization, make more efficient use of charitable resources and counter abuses.

To encourage fresh ideas and cost-effectiveness, voluntarists also wish to improve coordination with the statutory authorities and between charitable bodies. (How reminiscent of the late Victorians.) This is seen as particularly urgent at a time when politicians and civil servants are turning their minds increasingly to the crisis in the inner cities. The creation of stable urban communities has been perceived as the greatest challenge to philanthropists since the mid-nineteenth century, and traditionally, they have turned to local initiatives, which offer scope for participation and citizenship, as the best way forward. One contemporary idea is to create community trusts, well established in America, which would facilitate funding partnerships between local authorities, corporations and private donors. Another is for small societies to be registered with the local authorities, which would free the Charity Commission to get on with more pressing business. To the extent that remedies for social ills are sought in local communities, which are themselves often jealous of their autonomy, charitable effort is likely to be seen to play a more prominent part in the national life. Relatively free from unbending bureaucracy, voluntarists are well served by community projects and the theme that small is beautiful. This is a point that is not lost on the great national charities, for today more and more of their funds are spent in aid of small-scale voluntary initiatives.

Disenchanted with the evolution of post-war social policy, today's philanthropic advocates, whether they call themselves voluntarists, community workers or believers in welfare pluralism, are in expansive mood. Alienated by faceless bureaucracy and what many of them see as an erosion of personal freedom, officials of the National Council for Voluntary Organisations and other societies want nothing less than a revival of those charitable traditions in which citizens are seen as having duties as well as rights, in which personal service is valued and unfettered. Sometimes citing the 'Father of the Welfare State', William Beveridge, who sought a fruitful balance between statutory provision and self-help, they want voluntarism to play a larger and more effective role alongside government in the drive for social progress. In the spontaneous expression of personal service they see a training ground of good citizenship and the makings of a civilized society. In the quickening rise of *ad hoc* voluntary institutions they see participatory democracy and social integration at work, especially valued in the case of minorities and other deprived groups which are little represented politically. Not least, they see in the myriad forms of formal and casual philanthropy the free expression of individual moral values, especially needed in a society which has become increasingly secular. Their Victorian forebears, often criticized for sectarianism and seeming muddle, recognized the ambiguity in that well-worn phrase 'to help the poor to help themselves'. In our more prosperous and egalitarian society, where there are nearly as many volunteers as beneficiaries, it remains as ambiguous as ever.

II

Philanthropy ascendant

'We are just now overrun with philanthropy, and God knows where it will stop, or whither it will lead us', wrote the memoirist Charles Greville.[1] Though such melancholy doubts about the good men do one another were uttered from time to time in the early nineteenth century, they made little impression on a society increasingly confident that voluntary social action was the most reliable remedy for individual ills and social distress. Philanthropy, of course, had ancient traditions in Britain, as elsewhere; and while it is risky to attempt to measure its level between one period and another, the peculiar configuration of events taking place in the late eighteenth and early nineteenth centuries heightened and redirected British philanthropic impulses. Under the sway of social, religious and economic change, a new society was taking shape. The pressures of industrial development, rapid population growth and blighted cities enlivened charitable enterprise in a world relatively unadministered by the state. So too did the French Revolution and the suffering caused by the prolonged war with France, which coloured the lives of a generation. Invigorating piety and paternalism, war and revolution also deepened the conservative hue of the British philanthropic establishment.

Among the complex changes sweeping Britain in these years none was more important in its effects on philanthropy than religious revival. Christians of all denominations espoused charitable ideals, and few of them would dissent from the view that 'uncharitableness is that which strikes at the foundations of Christianity'.[2] Some denominations were more active in philanthropic causes than others, and most had particular charitable interests growing out of doctrinal interpretation and social circumstances.

But the rise of evangelicalism, or Bible Christianity, from the late eighteenth century onwards brought a new and vigorous emphasis to personal sacrifice and good works which had repercussions for people, whether they shared in the religious enthusiasm or not. To the faithful, even the most trivial charitable acts might be invested with symbolic significance. The general mood is captured in the writings of William Wilberforce and Hannah More, who reminded the higher classes of their social obligations in a time of political and social uncertainty. Like John Wesley, whose spiritual message reached humble people in distant corners of the kingdom, they argued that self-discipline and self-sacrifice were essential to liberty and social order. In evangelicalism, inside and outside the Church of England, there emerged an expression of individualist Christianity which allied faith, hope and charity to national purpose. Its most heralded campaign contributed to the abolition of the slave trade, a cause which illustrates the often blurred boundary between voluntary action and political reform.

Though narrow in its theology and often conservative in its politics, evangelicalism was wide in its sympathies. This 'vital religion' was intensely emotional and left its adherents obsessed with human depravity and the ideal of Christian perfection, whose very elusiveness animated conduct. Bible-centred, passages of scripture such as 'charity never faileth' and 'I was sick and ye visited me' had an awesome immediacy to those for whom works were a sign of redemption. The psychical turmoil which resulted from Christian self-examination predisposed the faithful to charitable conduct, in spite of the prevailing fatalistic attitude towards poverty which marked economic thinking after Malthus. The moral seriousness that underpinned the promotion of so many charitable causes in the nineteenth century, from anti-slavery to crèches, was conditioned by a degree of self-discipline that enlivened conscience and by the very restraints that religion placed on enjoyment and intellectual life. As that eminent twentieth-century Victorian G. M. Young remarked, 'Evangelical discipline, secularized as respectability, was the strongest binding force in a nation which without it might have broken up.'[3]

Like everyone else in the nineteenth century, evangelicals embraced the family as the paramount social institution. To most people, the home was not only a refuge from the cares of the world but a place of relative freedom. In the nineteenth century religion became increasingly domestic, one might say feminized, with many Christian rituals taking place in the privacy of the home. Family prayers and domestic meetings of wives, parishioners and servants encouraged the wider expression of familial kindness and neighbourliness. Dorcas meetings, for example, named after the woman of Joppa who made garments for the poor (Acts ix, 36) brought parishioners together in domestic sewing classes and prayer in aid of local causes or benighted heathens. A host of other institutions extended religious life from the home, church or chapel into the community, and not only for evangelicals. All faiths had a range of local charitable institutions such as visiting societies, mothers' meetings, and branches of national charities which combined welfare and missionary activities. For Catholics and Jews they were necessary if only to combat the proselytism of innumerable Protestant charities.

With its emphasis on the sanctity of family life, social pity and moral fervour, evangelicalism had the important side-effect of opening up greater opportunities for women in charitable service. Thought to be predisposed to religion and benevolence and given an education centred on home and family, women were well placed to take advantage of the possibilities in any extension of familial values to the community beyond the home. At home they had a recognized status and were able to carry out their domestic charities relatively free from formal constraints. From their domestic citadel, they made ever-wider forays into society as the front-line defenders of family life. Whether running a mothers' meeting, founding a refuge for prostitutes, or sitting on management committees of charities, they applied their domestic knowledge and spread the concerns of family and relations into the wider world. What may be described as an explosion of societies run by women took place in the nineteenth century, institutional expressions of a vital female culture with financial resources.[4] These charities not only brought issues such as child welfare and moral reform to the fore, but were to have a profound effect upon women's lives and expectations. Despite the altered circumstances of women's existence in the twentieth century, there is little sign that their enthusiasm or capacity for philanthropy has much abated. Many of the voluntary traditions of modern Britain are deeply rooted in female culture, which found a compelling, and relatively unrestricted, avenue for expression in charitable work.

The origins of the characteristic traditions of British voluntarism may also be detected in the particular affinity and mix of evangelicalism and liberalism which emerged in the nineteenth century against the background of the problems and opportunities created by industrial and demographic change. Evangelicalism harnessed social conscience to liberal doctrine. Much nineteenth-century philanthropy may be seen as liberalism turning its mind to social conditions under religious pressure. As the jurist Albert Dicey remarked, 'the appeal of the Evangelicals to personal religion corresponds with the appeal of Benthamite Liberals to individual energy'.[5] Both liberals and evangelicals, who were often one and the same, were ardent individualists. British Protestants increasingly assumed that individual behaviour determined spiritual progress, a view very much in tune with the *laissez-faire* ethos of the secular world in which material success corresponded to salvation. In the communion of Christianity and commerce, religious virtues resembled those of successful businessmen, with an echo of the Calvinist's suspicion of wealth, which encouraged giving some of it away. With few restrictions placed on charitable enterprise, it may be seen as the human face of capitalism, addressing the social and individual ills which capitalism often created or exacerbated. Competition for sinners and distress was a feature of nineteenth-century philanthropy. And in a society splintered by class, religious and local allegiances charities proliferated and competed.

With their deepseated belief in the value of the individual and the social value of individual conscience, evangelicals and liberals typically distrusted the state. Nonconformists had good historical reasons for doing so, and their emphasis on the freedom of religious sects evolved naturally in the direction of independent voluntary associations. Inspired by that central doctrine of the atonement, evangelicals, whether nonconformist or Anglican, assumed that the individual as fellow sufferer, not as ratepayer, was responsible for the cares of the world. The state was an artificial contrivance, necessary to defend British interests and to punish the wicked, but incapable of redemptive action. Recoiling from Caesar, they believed the key to social progress lay in longstanding parish and local traditions, free from London rule. In towns, villages or urban parishes, familial kindness and neighbourliness would ideally extend ever wider into the community bringing social harmony and, perhaps, the millennium. For liberals, philanthropy was a form of enlightened self-interest. John Stuart Mill elaborated its political significance: 'The only security against political slavery, is the check maintained over governors, by the diffusion of intelligence, activity, and public spirit among the governed.' Without the habit of spontaneous voluntary action, he added, citizens 'have their faculties only half developed'.[6] Such views reconciled the liberal belief in Treasury restraint with their conviction that social ills were removable. In much of this there was a consensus with Tory paternalists and the many female philanthropists who saw society as essentially organic, whose distrust of government interference in social matters and whose commitment to local voluntary initiative, if not to individualism, was often as great as that of liberals.

The British have always been most interested in what happens around their homes and streets, despite the sporadic outpouring of usually ill-informed public sympathy for national causes or foreigners in distress. Yet most of the historical writing about philanthropy has focused on prominent institutions, celebrated personalities and policies radiating from the centre. It has rarely done justice to the innumerable local institutions, the humdrum labour and the successions of daily life which typify voluntary experience. To fill out the picture of Lord Shaftesbury's largesse and the social philosophy of the Charity Organisation Society (COS), it is essential to look more closely at voluntarism at the level of the family, the parish or the community. As noted, this approach does justice to the importance of female philanthropy. It also illuminates casual benevolence, of rich and poor alike, which persisted into the industrial age. Moreover, those innumerable societies which saturated the country, often branches of large institutions, are best studied in their parochial context. Seen from the point of view of individuals and institutions little known to fame or fortune, the history of philanthropy looks somewhat different from the picture often presented.

One does not need to be Samuel Smiles to recognize that propping up the family and the neighbourhood with good works and a little self-help is often the only way of preventing their deterioration. Philanthropists in the past were well aware of this and raised the ideal of familial and parochial service to new heights in the nineteenth century. Traditionally, the parish provided an administrative principle, the unit in which tithes were collected for charitable purposes. From the Middle Ages it was also a complex moral world in which family and neighbours acquitted their social and religious obligations. The immediacy and familiarity of the parish bound the community together, rich and poor, in a web of kindness, obligation and expectation. Perhaps the desire to reinvigorate the bonds of parochial life was inevitable in a time of religious revival and increasing urban decay. (It continues to make an appeal in a world which has lost its religious moorings but which has not solved the urban crisis). The parochial ideal gained enormous support in the nineteenth century across the political and religious spectrum. Indeed, as the scale of the urban problem increased, the greater became the appeal of small neighbourhood organizations. Advocates of the Gothic Revival, for example, revived the image of the parish church on a green, so beloved by ecclesiastical authorities and church architects alike, which summed up a vision of community service and social harmony. The image was no less powerful for being out of touch with urban realities.

The proponents of parochial service recognized the truth in that cliché that charity begins at home, while assuming that the home was a school which taught the sympathies and skills necessary to perform good works in a wider sphere. Whatever one's station or trouble, the family was the first place to turn, a view which persists even in our more highly administered state. Large families were the norm in the nineteenth century and misfortune, childbirth, sickness and death called continually on familial charity and the kindness of friends and neighbours. Traditional forms of domestic charity such as lying-in visiting and the distribution of money to servants on the death of an employer were ways of protecting the life of the family and the extended family in an unpredictable, often calamitous world. Arguably the most important theme running through the history of philanthropy is the desire of the charitable to protect and to elevate the family and to extend the blessings of an idealized home life into the wider community.

Among the many subjects illuminated by a study of domestic and parish life is the charity of the poor to the poor. This is not to deny the importance of philanthropy as a relationship which reflects social inequalities, in which the wealthy contribute to causes in aid of the poor in expectation of some return on their investment. But as one nineteenth-century writer argued, it is a common mistake to assume that 'charity is a duty which belongs specially to the rich'.[7] Fellow feeling may be all the stronger among those whose own circumstances are subject to the same privations as their friends and neighbours. Reference to working-class philanthropy pays tribute to the humanity of the poor, which is sometimes forgotten by those who see the working classes primarily as victims. And it represents a challenge to those social historians, under the influence of Marxism, who see charity as an expression of class conflict, a means by which the middle classes confirm their status and power. When confronted with working-class philanthropists, these historians are likely to argue that they were artisans and tradesmen and not the 'real' working class, i.e. the oppressed. Alternatively, they discuss working-class 'sharing', which in their vocabulary is a world apart from 'charity' with its bourgeois and religious associations.[8] But in playing down working-class selflessness and Christian compassion they reduce those they wish to elevate to traditions of mutual obligation or naked self-interest.

Social stability in Britain has had perhaps as much to do with working-class charity and self-help as it has had to do with middle-class philanthropy. This is not to underestimate the importance of those social disciplines pressed on the poor from above in the nineteenth century, but to suggest that charity, self-help, a sense of reciprocal obligation, and a desire for social stability come naturally enough to most people, whatever their social station. Friedrich Engels, invariably hostile to middle-class philanthropy, remarked that 'although the workers cannot really afford to give charity on the same scale as the middle class, they are nevertheless more charitable in every way'.[9] To Engels, and others of differing political persuasions, the help provided by the poor to one another was the only means by which they managed to survive a crisis. He and Marx did not consider that this expression of working-class solidarity might work to prevent a revolution. But this point was appreciated by many of their contemporaries with greater experience of slum life, who were not blinded by a belief in the inevitability of social upheaval. 'It is largely this kindness of the poor to the poor', remarked an Edwardian cleric, 'which stands between our present civilization and revolution'.[10]

Though unostentatious and uncelebrated, the charity of the poor to the poor was, according to various observers, startling in its extent. A survey of rather more prosperous working-class families in the 1890s showed that half of them contributed funds to charity each week.[11] As with their social superiors, working-class philanthropy flowed from their own needs and aspirations. Though its range was considerable, its degree is impossible to measure with any precision. Formal subscription lists do not make differentiation between social classes easy, but the many entries such as 'working man', 'factory operative', and 'domestic servant' make it clear that the working classes were represented across a wide field of charitable activity, often in association with campaigns initiated by the upper classes. Sometimes their support reveals political motives, as in their subscriptions to the Loyal and Patriotic Fund to promote parliamentary reform in the run up to the Great Reform Bill, or to the fund to relieve the Tolpuddle Martyrs. Here were antidotes to the political purposes which voluntary donations were put to by the landed classes. Working-class contributions were also notable in the campaigns to relieve victims of the Lancashire Cotton Famine, veterans of foreign wars and the voluntary hospitals. In several hospitals in the north of England, workmen provided well over half the income. In London and the Home Counties, the League of Mercy (1899), an auxiliary of the King Edward's Hospital Fund for London (1897), collected working-class subscriptions as a first priority. By 1947, when it was wound up, it had given £600,000 to the London hospitals alone.[12]

Much working-class charity was of the type applauded by Engels, local, spontaneous and independent, which rarely leaves a trace behind in the records: caring for ageing relatives, assisting kin in times of adversity, the provision of Sunday dinners, visiting sick friends, taking in washing, helping with rent, or dropping a coin in a hat at the local voluntary centre, the pub, to support an unemployed neighbour or someone who had lost a purse. Such actions, in which women often played the dominant role, were commonplaces in the day-to-day, unadministered lives of the poor. They help to explain why so many of the unemployed in the past never entered the workhouse or became paupers. So too do the more formal and therefore more often recorded charitable activities carried out by the working classes: setting up soup kitchens in emergencies (witness the recent example of the miners' strike of 1984), teaching Sunday school or ragged-school classes, running a Dorcas meeting or a boot club, joining a visiting or temperance society. Examples could be cited of working-class men and women who founded orphanages, ragged schools, navvy missions, homes for the disabled, refuges for prostitutes, washhouses, and district visiting charities. Could the Salvation Army, the Ragged School Union, the Guilds of Help or countless less celebrated institutions have operated without the financial support and unflagging industry of men and women drawn from the nation's humbler classes? And what of the voluntary traditions of Robert Owen's 'villages of cooperation' and the cooperative movement, now coming back into the welfare debate, which combined charity and mutual aid?

The respectable working class, often identified with church and chapel, was particularly noticeable in its charitable activity. (Evangelical dissent was especially attractive to the upwardly mobile, whatever their background.) Philanthropy was a test of respectability, and one had to be far down the social ladder, on poor relief or a recipient of charity, to be altogether free from social obligation. According to the standard Christian commentaries and many a sermon, the poor should accept their lowly station; but if they walked humbly and acted charitably they were promised 'the same heavenly inheritance' as the God-fearing rich. As a labourer from Northumberland remarked in the 1850s, 'the penalty for not helping one's neighbour is death, for it is a sin against God'.[13] Such sentiments were part of a Bible Christian's spiritual baggage and resulted in considerable working-class support for religious charities, many of them with a welfare role. Whether members of a church or chapel or supporters of a middle-class institution headquartered in London, the respectable poor contributed large sums in small amounts to the nineteenth-century missionary societies, domestic missions and related causes. While some of this support was extracted by pressure from social superiors or employers, most of it came naturally enough from working-class impulses and aspirations. Through Sunday schools and missionary societies, temperance and moral reform, mothers' meetings and visiting societies, working-class volunteers made connections with the wider world and integrated into the social system.

Participation in philanthropic causes was a sign of social status and social ambition, but it was also a part of the pattern of working-class education and leisure. To many, it was as important as the formal training picked up in charity schools or mechanics' institutes. In encouraging skills and a wider social outlook, it was not unlike the education on offer in mutual aid societies, such as trade unions and benefit clubs, which, it should be said, often had a charitable function. (The distinction between a philanthropic society and a mutual aid society is less clear cut than is sometimes assumed.) Whether in their own charities or working for middle-class institutions, working men and women honed a basic education and often developed skills in book-keeping, secretarial work, publicity and general organization. Such a training was a feature of most charities, whether they depended on volunteers or paid staff. (It proved particularly useful to middle-class women whose job prospects and educational opportunities were restricted.) For women and working men, charitable work opened up new interests, built up practical experience, self-confidence and self-respect. It was an expression of their personal freedom as autonomous individuals. In voluntary societies, unlike the wider world over which they had little control, they could make choices and decisions which had meaning for their own lives and the lives of others. In the context of the British political transformation taking place in the nineteenth and early twentieth centuries the view that charitable work represents a 'nursery school of democracy' is especially apt.

Cooperative benevolence, in which respectable working men and women joined their social superiors in a charitable society, is a distinctive, though little studied, tradition in Britain. Like the casual benevolence of the poor its extent is impossible to gauge, and one should not exaggerate its effects, but in the nineteenth century it was much valued by the philanthropic establishment. 'Poor contributions,' announced one Christian magazine, 'whether we consider the proportion which they bear to the whole wealth of the givers, or their aggregate amount are, in effect, beyond all comparison the most important.'[14] Such contributions, whether in aid of local hospitals or foreign missions, were easier to elicit in those communities with a resident middle class and declined in those cities where a geographical gulf increasingly separated rich and poor. But they suggest that the middle classes did not insensitively impose their will on their poorer neighbours but often worked with them or through them in line with local opinion and conditions. The relationships which developed between volunteers in charities which were socially heterogeneous took on a moral character (just as the relationship between the charitable and the beneficiary often did). In the immediate, face-to-face world of the parish, it often reinforced paternalism in the higher classes and deference in the lower, but it was often a sign of shared values and a common culture. We must put aside twentieth-century assumptions of social democracy if we are to understand the character and implications of charitable cooperation in a society in which social hierarchy and a sense of place were so deeply ingrained.

Many of the aforementioned themes may be illustrated by reference to the operations of particular charities. In the early nineteenth century one of the most influential institutions which encouraged the development of a common culture, cooperation between the classes and the idea of parochial service was the Society for Bettering the Condition and Increasing the Comforts of the Poor (SBCP). Founded in 1796 by Thomas Bernard, William Wilberforce and other leading philanthropists, it was one of the most innovative institutions of its day, or any other. As a forum for ideas and a clearing house of information on new projects it may be seen as an early 'coordinating' charity. The Society became synonymous with Bernard (1750–1818), and while it survived him its influence waned after his death. A lawyer turned philanthropist, whose father was the last Royal Governor of Massachusetts, he has been called 'a capital example of the philanthropic impulse in a singularly pure form' and 'perhaps the representative English philanthropist of the age of the French Revolution'.[15]

Bernard developed a philosophy of charity which drew its strength from the good sense and industry of the poor themselves, and in an age of evangelical enthusiasm and counter revolution he remained remarkably balanced. He was more concerned with promoting effective remedies for poverty than with perpetuating the status quo in the name of patriotism. A latitudinarian Anglican, his practical and liberal cast of mind, probably heightened by his days at Harvard, freed his philanthropy from the calculated benevolence that is often associated with anti-Jacobinism in Britain. While he had close ties with the Clapham sect of evangelicals, his philanthropy was rather less preoccupied with religious conversion and the reformation of working-class manners and morals. The SBCP did not act as a form of moral police designed to render the criminal code unnecessary. It proposed to convert and to educate the irreligious, but typical of the day these objects were interwoven with the relief of distress and the promotion of social reform. Along with many other charitable agencies which might be cited, it may be seen as an antidote to the view of historians such as E. P. Thompson, who argue that the British 'humanitarian tradition became warped beyond recognition' in the years 1790–1830.[16]

For two decades Bernard compiled the Society's *Reports* and wrote their thoughtful introductions, which illuminated a storehouse of useful and practical information. Virtually everything which affected the happiness of the poor appeared, including discussions of education, parish relief, friendly societies, cooperative stores, soup kitchens, provident institutions, prisons, hospitals, workhouses, libraries, cottage gardens, coal mines, and factory life. Some of the schemes recommended seem curious today, among them the many recipes for ox head soup, but many of the Society's ideas became part of the stock-in-trade of philanthropy. In his preliminary address, Bernard called for the study of the poor to be made a science, a theme which has been prominent in the history of philanthropy since the late eighteenth century. Like the utilitarian Jeremy Bentham and the American scientist Count Rumford, his ideal was the application of the empirical method to social conditions. Scornful of vague benevolence, he demanded detailed study of specific projects if charity was to produce the desired results. A belief, which he shared with Robert Owen, that environment was largely responsible for the formation of character, lay behind his respect for the labouring classes. As with so much philanthropic activity which followed, his object was to promote charitable projects which would transform the environment, especially the home environment, and thus encourage moral improvement and self-help. The realization of Bernard's plans depended on the benevolence of the poor themselves.

An underlying theme in the *Reports* of the SBCP was the crucial importance of parish life and parochial service. Several of Bernard's interests betray a nostalgia for a pre-revolutionary, pre-industrial world of more settled social relationships. But whether reporting on a working-class visiting charity in West London or describing parochial relief in an agricultural district, he assumed that a sense of place was essential to human happiness. In his day the poor law, insufficiently financed and badly administered, left a legacy of class tension, particularly noticeable in the countryside. Instead of driving the poor into workhouses, Bernard wanted parish relief to encourage industry and familial responsibility, for the worst home environment he thought preferable to a workhouse. In line with this he sponsored ladies' associations which took up the cause of educating and employing the female poor. (The percentage of female subscribers to the SBCP rose dramatically in the first decade of the nineteenth century.) His object was to give the labouring classes an idea that they had an interest in parish life. Thus the main thrust of this campaign for social improvement flowed from the promotion of small-scale preventive measures of self-help and voluntary action which he chronicled in the *Reports*. Ideally, these schemes would result in working-class families being able to support themselves without recourse to the poor law. Keeping families intact and free from dependence on the ratepayer was the central plank of nineteenth-century social policy.

Bernard believed that local charitable agencies were best suited to relieve distress, but he was not hostile to government legislation to redress particular abuses. Anti-slavery, exploited chimney sweeps and poor industrial apprentices were examples where he looked to the state to complement philanthropy. Sir Robert Peel's Act of 1802, for example, which limited the hours and improved the treatment of apprentices in cotton mills, was framed by a committee consisting largely of members of the SBCP. Bernard, who took a keen interest in factory reform, saw the Act's defects and pressed for tougher legislation. In 1805, he wrote, 'I trust the manufacturer will on his part concede that it is *the duty of the state* to watch over his extended speculations – and to ascertain that his mills and factories are not converted into *seminaries of disease, of misery, and profligacy*.'[17] These remarks were worthy of Lord Shaftesbury, who in the next generation would carry forward Bernard's campaigns on behalf of factory workers and chimney sweeps. Neither man envisaged a time when government action would render philanthropy the 'junior partner' in social reform. It would be difficult to turn Bernard into a forerunner of the Welfare State, but he recognized that there was room for public as well as private initiative in softening the hardships associated with the nation's transition from an agricultural economy to an urban and industrial one.

The SBCP had a strong rural orientation, but even in that charity's heyday urban industrial life posed many of the most intractable problems for philanthropists. (This was perhaps less obvious to them than to us looking back on the period.) Many cities were growing at an alarming rate. In Manchester and Salford, for example, population rose by 45 per cent in a single decade, 1821–31. The pressure of population, which doubled in England and Wales in the first half of the nineteenth century, combined with the breaking up of familiar social patterns to create a distressing level of pauperism and social dislocation. Concentrated in the nation's cities, the suffering was also highly visible in town and countryside. Traditional forms of charity such as endowed trusts, almsgiving and casual visiting were inadequate to meet the growing demands. In overcrowded cities knowledge of hardship was more difficult to come by than in the countryside, and it was less easy to distinguish between real and feigned distress. Fresh responses were needed to cope with these and related issues. The demand was such that it called increasingly on the support of the public at large and not simply the benefactions of isolated individuals.

The government's response to the social question in these years was an investigation into the operations of the existing poor laws and the passing of the Poor Law Amendment Act of 1834. Though cautiously implemented, a guiding principle of the Act was the abolition of outdoor relief to the able-bodied. Hard work and Spartan provision were to be the norm in workhouses for the most destitute. As desired, the Act resulted in a drop in the rates. The effect of it on charities is not altogether clear, but as a 'charter of the ratepayer' it may have stimulated contributions. A clarification of the respective spheres of philanthropy and the state emerged, though it was highly artificial. It was tacitly agreed that charity was to assist deserving cases, those who could be helped by preventive or remedial action; the poor law would cope with undeserving paupers. There was to be little, if any, overlapping of authority; charity was to begin where public relief ended. This conventional wisdom was ritually espoused, most notably in later years by the COS, but it did not describe the reality on the ground. State institutions and voluntary bodies were never so compartmentalized. It was not always easy to distinguish between the deserving and undeserving; and philanthropists, often hostile to the poor law, pursued paupers indoors. They were reluctant to give up anyone as lost this side of the grave, however undeserving. The Workhouse Visiting Society (1858) alone sent thousands of volunteers into workhouses to console inmates and to make life a little less brutish. Despite complaints about over-zealous and meddling volunteers, the authorities let them in. It was often good public relations, and economical, to do so.

If central government's reluctance to spend money on social problems was a stimulus to philanthropy, so too was the relative weakness of local government during most of the nineteenth century. In the rapidly changing, and for many deteriorating, social environment it fell to a host of voluntary societies to intervene in the relationship between benefactors and the needy. They took up the challenge with alacrity. Modelled on established charities such as the Society for Promoting Christian Knowledge (1698), they were financed by subscriptions and governed by committees. Some, like the SBCP, were set up for general social and moral improvement; many others dealt with specific problems or distresses. Some were large well-funded societies with associated branches around the country, a form of organization pioneered by the missionary societies. But most were small parish-based charities with little or no support outside their immediate communities. By the mid-nineteenth century these various institutions, which represent the form of charitable organization most familiar to us today, were so ubiquitous that Greville could complain about the nation being 'overrun' by them.

What most distinguished the voluntary societies from endowed trusts, which had been so important to eighteenth-century philanthropy, was their public nature and their consequent need for advertising and effective public relations. Dependent on the support of patrons and subscribers, the voluntary societies required public approval for the cause in question. The slightest hint of impropriety could bring public disapproval and a consequent loss of funds. Continually in the public eye, they had to carry the public with them if a change in object were to be undertaken. Unlike endowed trusts, there were few legal restraints imposed on 'collecting' charities. But answerable to their public as they were, the societies had to put on the best possible public face in their various functions and annual reports, which set out their aims and chronicled their successes. Often included in the reports were long lists of subscribers, still a feature of many voluntary societies. They were an economical version of those church plaques which celebrate benevolent parishioners and had the same ulterior purpose, to encourage further patronage. As the reports reveal, fund-raising was an obsession, requiring ever more ingenious methods.

Like charities before and after, the voluntary societies of the early and mid-nineteenth century reflected the preoccupations of benevolent individuals as well as objective social conditions. To those of a philanthropic disposition, charitable motives may be independent of social and economic conditions, though they often accommodate to them. Thus many charities, including the Peace Society (1816) and the RSPCA (1824), had only an indirect connection with those physical distresses associated with urban and industrial life. One reason for this was that human suffering was commonly seen through a religious lens; in a time when medicine dealt largely with prognosis and could do little to restore patients' bodies, this becomes more understandable. Many ardent Christians, though sensitive to disease and social malaise, were more anxious to save souls than bodies. In concentrating souls, the urban environment offered them opportunities for proselytizing. Many of the largest nineteenth-century charities, such as the missionary, tract and Bible societies took up this challenge. And many other institutions with a more obvious welfare role, such as visiting societies and refuges for prostitutes, typically had a strong missionary element. But wherever philanthropists were to be found, they desired to extend familial values through voluntary action. In Britain, they sought to reform the family through a moral and physical cleansing of the nation's homes. Abroad, they held out to the benighted the model of the free and happy British family, ennobled by Christianity's domestic qualities.

Ironically for a society which placed such a premium on the promotion of family life, there was a growing institutionalization of particular sections of the community in residential charities in the nineteenth century. This posed a dilemma, and one which remains when so many people continue to be taken into care. Of course, many of the people who wound up in institutions previously lived precarious lives outside any household structure and had no extended family to fall back on. For all the disadvantages, a charitable society looked more promising to them than a workhouse or a prison. Thousands of prostitutes fell into this category and voluntarily entered refuges or Magdalene homes, which rapidly increased in number in the Victorian years when philanthropic women turned their attention to the issue of social purity. Others, the most awkward cases for the authorities, had families in a state of disintegration, and it was thought preferable to save them from further familial violence and social abuse by withdrawing them from their homes. Thousands of boys and girls were committed to reformatories, orphanages, or asylums of one sort or another where they were given a rudimentary education. Many people felt that they were a drain on their families and entered institutions which catered to their particular needs or social background. Thousands of aged widows took this option. But whatever form the institution took it was likely to pride itself on recreating a domestic atmosphere or operating on the 'family system'. (This was particularly suitable for young females, who so often became domestic servants.) So powerful was the image of the happy home that even when the family had failed, a familial model sustained the benevolent in their beliefs. Yet calling their institutions 'homes' was often little more than a subtle deceit, used as much to salve their own consciences as to address the problem at hand.

Among the first to be segregated into homes and schools were the handicapped, particularly blind and deaf children. Today, such quasi-medical charities are among the best funded in Britain. The reasons for the emergence of specialized charities offering care and training for the disabled are obscure, but the combination of economic prosperity, new methods of treatment, and Christian conscience especially moved by the suffering of children help to explain it. So too does the ethic of the day which could not bear to see any individual dependent on others, even someone disabled; and which often assumed that children with physical handicaps were prone to criminal behaviour. The blind had aroused benevolence for centuries, but only in the 1790s did institutional training become available in England, first in Liverpool with its School for the Indigent Blind (1790). The deaf had not attracted nearly so much attention as the blind, but the first charity offering them special facilities opened in Bermondsey in 1783. By 1860 there were sixteen charities in London dealing with the blind and the deaf and about three times that number in the provinces.[18] As with so many societies with costly overheads, they were typically supported by wealthy patrons with personal, or familial, experience of the affliction in question.

One of the fastest growing forms of charitable enterprise in the first half of the nineteenth century was the residential institution whose beneficiaries were from the higher classes, typically in reduced circumstances or suffering from particular diseases. These charities are difficult to classify, but they were a reflection of the increased disposable income available to the well-to-do. Some philanthropists saw them as a sound investment when so much money was being expended, often to little effect, on less socially acceptable claimants. Many of them emerged to care for the insane or to cater to particular professions. The Retreat at York, founded by the Society of Friends for the mentally disturbed 'of all ranks', is one example; Morden College in Blackheath, a home for necessitous merchants founded in the seventeenth century, is another.[19] While the funding of such institutions was generous, the conditions of entry were stringent and once inside the code of behaviour demanding. (In the nineteenth century the moral code increasingly resembled that which obtained in evangelical families.) Often in unfamiliar surroundings and subject to moralizing and petty regulation, the genteel inmate must have felt some of the humiliation that the poor often complained about in institutions for their care and improvement.

Most charities which the higher classes organized for themselves were less restrictive; many of them resembled mutual aid societies or provident funds and simply provided pensions to registered members. The National Benevolent Institution (1812) alone granted nearly £200,000 to indigent gentlemen and professionals in its first fifty years, much of it paid out of legacies bequeathed by the well-to-do.[20] Sampson Low, who catalogued the charities of London in the mid-nineteenth century, discovered seventy-two such professional funds, not including twenty for clergymen and Dissenting ministers. The growth of such funds, particularly those for naval and military officers and their families, may have been stimulated by the reforms which gradually reduced the number of Crown pensioners. Among others, licensed victuallers, decayed governesses, Old Etonians, and wives of deceased London doctors enjoyed societies for their support. Aged ladies made a particularly powerful demand on charitable revenues, then as now, if only because of their survival rate. But running out of relatives was a hazardous business for everyone, and the wise took precautions whenever possible.

By mid-century the range of charitable activity between and among the social classes was phenomenal. Institutions were under way for virtually every human ill, individual or social, moral or physical, many of them associated with the increasingly urban and industrial environment. The historian Sir James Stephen, writing in the late 1840s, called the period the age of charitable societies: 'For the cure of every sorrow . . . there are patrons, vice-presidents and secretaries. For the diffusion of every blessing . . . there is a committee.'[21] Despite reservations about the organization and accomplishments of voluntary effort, few doubted that it was the surest hedge against misfortune and indispensable to social progress. Thus there were enormous pressures on individuals of all ranks to contribute time and money to charitable causes. In this atmosphere, the financial resources of philanthropy, which far exceeded the gross expenditure on poor relief, expanded each year. As men, women and children joined charities in unprecedented numbers, so too did the human resources. There were many people who shirked their philanthropic duty; others who did it out of pure self-interest. For those diverse Christians who set the tone of Victorian life, and not only the middle classes, duty turned to privilege. Elizabeth Barrett Browning, who honoured their code of service and self-sacrifice in *Aurora Leigh*, put it simply:

> After Christ, work turns to privilege;
> And henceforth one with our humanity.[22]

III

Parochial service in practice

If the first half of the nineteenth century saw philanthropy ascendant, the second half witnessed its triumph. The Victorians' confidence that philanthropy could cope with the dimensions of distress baffles us today. But in their little administered parochial world, social ills had great immediacy. Here the pressures were individual, and they saw few alternatives beyond benevolence and self-help. As suggested, women felt the pressure to contribute to local causes particularly, for their lives were wrapped up more often in their neighbourhoods and given over to serving family and friends. In the familiarity of the community, whether rural or urban, benevolence was a moral obligation, if not a test of faith. It found expression in the best of times as in the worst, which helps to explain why the prosperous mid-Victorian years were a philanthropic golden age. The results were sometimes disproportionate to the need of the recipient, but proportionate to the need of the giver. In Victorian Britain, a sense of duty to the community outstripped the assertion of rights to social assistance on the part of the deprived.

Recreating the world of Victorian local charity is a problem because so many of the institutions, once so familiar, are now largely forgotten. But the more deeply one looks into the subject the richer it becomes. Through the Charity Commissioners we can trace the array of charitable endowments, often for schools, almshouses and doles for the poor, that were such a feature of pre-industrial parish life. The array of local voluntary institutions, often interrelated and mutually supporting, are more obscure because their records, when they exist, are often incomplete. They varied in character with the needs of each community; increasingly, they were auxiliaries of national charities, but many remained wholly autonomous bodies. Membership numbers varied from under ten to hundreds. Women far exceeded men in their willingness to participate and several of the most important parish charities were female institutions altogether, to which men, clerics prominent among them, were invited to say prayers or to give support. Typified by the mothers' meeting, which will be discussed in detail, these female organizations usually involved needlework. At the heart of female culture in the nineteenth century, sewing was crucial to women's philanthropy. Vital to the domestic economy, it merged with female piety and signified those feminine ideals of home, family, and respectability. It suggested love for others.

By the end of the nineteenth century most communities of any size with a mixed social make-up would have boasted working parties, Dorcas meetings, mothers' meetings, Bible societies and temperance societies, which met in homes, churches or chapels, or in mission rooms rented for the occasion. Also common were other voluntary bodies which had specific welfare functions, such as lying-in and maternity charities, blanket clubs, coal clubs, medical clubs, sick benefit societies and advice bureaux with a poor man's lawyer (the Salvation Army was a pioneer of the latter). Often such agencies were attached to city missions, district-visiting societies or mothers' meetings. Innumerable penny banks, savings banks, provident clubs, goose clubs, and slate clubs, which reflected the Victorian obsession with thrift and mutual aid, were also attached to charities. The obsession with sin was common to many of the above-mentioned institutions, but in the late nineteenth century many parishes had also their own societies devoted to social purity or moral reform, often in association with national charities. One fascinating institution was the 'fathers' meeting', an offshoot of the mothers' meeting, which took for its object the reformation of husbands. The young were richly served by Sunday schools, juvenile branches of missionary or Bible societies, Bands of Hope, ragged schools, lending libraries, Bible classes, boot clubs, barefoot missions, clothing clubs, milk schemes, penny dinner societies, holiday clubs, and sewing classes, which boys sometimes attended. Nor were children excluded from the organizations of adults, for if the habits of benevolence and self-help were to be passed from generation to generation it was wise to set an example to the young.

Of the many forms of local benevolence that came into prominence in Britain by the mid-nineteenth century, none was more important than district visiting.[1] It represented the charitable world's most significant contribution to relieving the nation's perennial ills, especially in their urban manifestation. It may be seen as the essential institution reflecting that parochial idealism which grew in proportion to the pains of urban society. It should also be seen against that background of opinion, discussed earlier, which was suspicious of government intervention in social matters, hostile to mounting poor rates, and anxious to preserve local autonomy. Gaining enormous public support, the visiting movement was so widespread by the end of the nineteenth century that few of Britain's inhabitants could have been unaware of its existence, certainly not the poor whose homes were canvassed, sometimes invaded, so assiduously. Where thoroughly applied, it was a system of investigation and relief, increasingly influenced by social science, that would have warmed the heart of Jeremy Bentham. What it added to utilitarianism was the personal, Christian concern for individual suffering. The simple doctrine which informed visiting, and so many other charitable causes, was that social outcasts could only be saved by the agency of another decent human being, who cared enough about them to be interested in the issue of their survival.

Geared to cities, the visiting societies were usually based on parish boundaries. (In Victorian London a typical parish would have from 4,000 to 6,000 inhabitants, but the poorest parishes had twice these numbers.) Dividing neighbourhoods into districts, they assigned volunteers, usually women, to specific streets and households. Ideally there would be one visitor to every twenty to forty families, but this was rarely achieved in the poorest neighbourhoods. With weekly visits, or more often if the need arose, it brought the face-to-face charity of the country village to city slums. This was in line with the thinking of Bernard and the Scottish philanthropist Thomas Chalmers, who hoped that with smaller units the poor could be given the type of help which would bring out their self-reliance. The objects of visiting were straightforward: the prevention of distress and the promotion of family life and social harmony. (In practice as much time was spent on patching up as on prevention.) The means of achieving these ambitious aims were less obvious, though everyone agreed that the best way to sanctify the family was to work through it by personal ministration. Few other philanthropic forms were so well suited to that persistent moral and social imperative, the defence of family life.

The most imaginative visiting schemes were devised by religious agencies, sometimes representing a single denomination, sometimes inter- or non-denominational. They emerged out of a rich tradition. Enjoined by scripture and practised by deacons in the Early Church, visiting the poor had been carried out by churchmen and others for centuries. The Methodists were among the first to make visiting a regular feature of church organization (the movement is often dated to the founding of the Methodist Strangers' Friend Society in 1785), but in time all faiths became involved in the organization of visiting. Some societies were large and looked into a wide range of distresses. The General Society for Promoting District Visiting (1828), for example, had 573 visitors by 1832. Others were smaller and targeted particular groups, such as Jews, dockers or gypsies. Others still isolated particular problems, such as the infirm, the aged or the blind. (There were forty-five visiting charities to the blind alone by 1889, the pioneers in social work among the blind.)[2] Some of them were run by the aristocracy and the gentry, most by the middle classes, and not a few by the poor themselves. In London at least, clerks, tradesmen and artisans were more likely to be visitors than gentlemen. But with few exceptions, the societies were heavily dependent on the willingness of women to come forward as volunteers. And as with so many other forms of philanthropy, there was often a mingling of the classes in the societies. As the century progressed, more and more visiting agencies used working-class men and women, often paid employees, as a way of penetrating the worst neighbourhoods.

Whether a visiting society was attached to a city-wide mission, a church or chapel, or simply a local body assembled by concerned residents, the parochial ideal was central to it. It was impossible to recreate the idealized social bonds of a village parish in city slums with shifting populations, but the benefits of visiting could be and often were considerable, not only to the beneficiary. These benefits varied with the condition of the community, the nature of the charity, and, not least, the character of the individual visitor. We should not assume in our secular age that the religious message often on offer was meaningless to the visited. The many letters from them cited in the charitable records suggest that many humble people, particularly the old and sick, received consolation from the prayers, Bible readings and long hours spent over their individual souls. But visitors prone to moralizing were often turned away at the door. (Doorstep politics grew up in the age of district-visiting, and many a party canvasser learned lessons from it.) Most visitors, even those with essentially a religious message, delivered the homilies with a basket of material necessities wrapped in domestic advice. While many philanthropists thought that carrying a Bible in one hand and a basket of food in the other was undesirable, it was a compromise which kept many a door from being slammed in the face. The COS, among other institutions, avoided this danger by accepting the principle that volunteers should receive permission to visit.[3]

A visiting society's range of services depended, of course, on its aims and finances. They commonly offered food, recipes, coals, clothing, blankets, tracts, Bibles, a sympathetic ear, and assistance on matters of domestic importance, such as sanitation and child care. The distribution of money, which some societies permitted, came increasingly under attack in the nineteenth century as it was widely thought to encourage pauperism. Collecting money from families for rent payments or furniture was more common. Visitors also built up and disseminated a wealth of local information, intermixed with gossip, which was often very useful to the community. (This service is now little provided outside the corner shop.) Visitors were often well placed to put employers, particularly of domestic servants, in contact with potential employees. They provided a check on absenteeism from work and truancy from school. (The latter became more important after the introduction of state education in 1870.) Putting their charges in touch with evening classes, mothers' meetings and Sunday schools was another feature of their work. They also served the community by referring the undefended to advice bureaux and the sick to local doctors and dispensaries. Many district-nursing associations grew directly out of district visiting. Visitors provided introductions to other charitable societies, who might be able to provide assistance in individual cases. And with time they kept in closer touch with poor law officials as well, which could help to keep their charges out of the workhouse. The workhouse symbolized failure to the charitable as well as to the inmate.

The motives of district visitors, like philanthropists generally, were complex. For many volunteers, whether in a parish charity or in a national campaign, religious motives were paramount. Much benevolence was simply a result of an acceptance of a social teaching of the churches or biblical prescriptions to be charitable. As suggested earlier, it was often a product of spiritual anxiety, a preoccupation with sin and salvation. This anxiety was conditioned by evangelical theology, which increasingly rejected the predestinarian views of Calvin. In positing a measure of free will, Wesley, Wilberforce and others encouraged the view that salvation was conditional and provisional. In the lives of evangelicals this meant that spiritual doubts lingered on after they believed their conversions to have taken place. Many of those whose 'hearts yearned for sinners' visited the poor or pursued their other charities not only in anticipation of grace but in fear of backsliding and damnation. When they proselytized on their visiting rounds, they were also looking into their own souls and trying to resolve those conflicts born of self-examination. To glimpse how spiritual 'heart burning' might trigger benevolent action, one must try to enter the mind of an evangelical, for whom eternal fire was not a metaphor but a prospect. The mid-century diary of Mary Cryer, the wife of a Methodist missionary, is typical of hundreds of others:

> I find the cross in canvassing from door to door for Missions, and perhaps not succeeding in one case in twenty; I find it still more in begging for a poor starving fellow-creature, and perhaps now and then meeting with a chilling repulse; . . . but, most of all, I find it in going from door to door on the visiting plan, trying to persuade sinners to attend God's house, and flee from the wrath to come . . . But O, when I have to make my own way, and meet the cold looks and even the rude rebuff of those who will not be subdued by kindness and courtesy, then nature does shrink; . . . Yet I dare not give it up: it is God's work; He is with us in it, and we have some little fruit . . . I often think I ought not to be reckoned among the

soldiers, till I burn with a nobler, warmer, bolder spirit, for the fulfilment of His love's redeeming plan.[4]

In the day-to-day life of the community, we can detect a variety of philanthropic motives which were as compelling as religion and not irreconcilable with it. The pressures to contribute were certainly considerable and not easily dismissed in surroundings both stark and familiar. Yet the pleasures and advantages of charitable work were what made it irresistible to many volunteers. The weekly round among the poor, though often harrowing, could be a source of immense pleasure for those with time for it. To be needed, to be counted upon, to be called 'dear' or 'friend', was a great reward. This was especially so for those with their own family problems. As the Master of Balliol, Benjamin Jowett, wrote to Florence Nightingale: 'Do you ever observe how persons take refuge from family unhappiness in philanthropy?'[5] For those without families, familiarity with their needy neighbours also could be a great attraction. One visitor, who went on to become the first Principal of Newnham College, remarked: 'The children know me, and speak my name. This was delicious to me, and worth more than a thousand praises.'[6] Parish work gave the benevolent status in the community, which for women at least was in short supply elsewhere. Whether visiting one's own parish or 'slumming' in distant neighbourhoods, it broke the domestic routine. The dinner, bazaar or fête which capped a society's annual labour also broke the monotony. Such activities confirm that philanthropic work was not simply a result of the Christian duty of self-denial, though that was often an important part of it. It represented basic human impulses: to be useful, to be seen to be useful, to be respectable, to be informed, to be amused, to 'keep up with the Joneses', to gossip, to wield power, to love and be loved. Middle-class guilt, a feature of our more egalitarian age, was a much less prominent philanthropic motive in a time of accepted social hierarchy.

By the mid-nineteenth century, district-visiting had marshalled a vast army of volunteers addressing themselves to the administration of relief in Britain. But the more they investigated, the more distress they uncovered. How could the health and happiness of the poorest classes best be promoted in those congested and infested slums that blackened the nation's reputation? (The Salvation Army (1865) and settlements such as Toynbee Hall (1884) would eventually provide distinctive philanthropic answers.) In many working-class communities there were few established philanthropic traditions, apart from the charity of the poor to the poor, and funds and volunteers were difficult to come by. Social science techniques grafted on to church organization held out some hope, but there was always a need for experimentation, especially in administration. Among the most innovative and important visiting schemes, though little remembered today, were those which emerged in London in the mid-nineteenth century. These included the London City Mission (1835) which pioneered work among minorities, and the Metropolitan Visiting and Relief Association (1843) which was a federation of parish visiting societies.

Perhaps the most notable experiments in visiting were initiated by the Ranyard Mission.[7] Founded by Ellen Ranyard in 1857, it was a peculiarly Victorian response to the problems of urban life. Using ingenious methods, it succeeded in penetrating the most appalling London neighbourhoods, where disease and irreligion were rife and where an overcrowded population threatened to overwhelm the means of subsistence. Mrs Ranyard (1810–75) was born in Nine Elms, the daughter of a cement maker. Raised as a nonconformist, she had been a visitor to the poor from childhood; and like many other philanthropists, it was her personal experience as a visitor (one of her friends died of a fever after an outing among the poor) which stimulated her life-long interest in philanthropy. With a particular concern for the lives of poor women, she developed the idea of the 'Bible woman'. This paid missionary cum social worker, a working-class woman drawn from the neighbourhood to be canvassed, was to provide the 'missing link' between the poorest families and their social superiors. Another distinctive feature introduced by Mrs Ranyard was the use of middle-class superintendents, usually from outside the district, to administer the programme, pay the salaries of the Bible women and supervise the mothers' meetings which were held each week in rented mission rooms. Such ideas were designed to meet the especial needs of inner-city neighbourhoods, where middle-class residents were in short supply. By 1867, there were 234 Bible women working across the metropolis and the idea had been adopted by various charities outside London. Given a three-month training by the Mission in the poor law, hygiene, and scripture, Mrs Ranyard's agents sought to turn the city's outcast population into respectable, independent citizens through an invigoration of family life. They represented the first corps of paid social workers in England.[8]

Using the postal districts, the Mission mapped out London's streets, courts, and alleys and assigned the Bible women to their own neighbourhoods. Familiarity with a district was thought essential if the immediacy of parish life was to be recreated in the bowels of London. Being local, the Bible women could walk about their districts inconspicuously, though they were occasionally insulted and some of them had buckets of slop thrown over them. From the beginning, the Mission instructed the Bible women to sell Bibles and to provide domestic advice to wives and mothers. It was argued that the reform of mothers was the most crucial task if the condition of the poor was to be improved. Selling Bibles was found to be much easier when combined with tips on cooking, cleaning, and other household matters. Before long, the poor subscribed to schemes to pay for clothing, coals, food and furniture. The Bible women raised the considerable sum of £44,000 from the poor, mostly for clothing and furniture, in the Mission's first decade.[9] Inducements to providence were a feature of most visiting charities, and Mrs Ranyard demanded that nothing be provided that was not paid for. Alert to the dangers of indiscriminate relief, she wished to give every encouragement to self-help. Self-help was social gospel to Victorian philanthropists, and the Ranyard Mission's successes in this sphere were greeted with enthusiasm by the charitable establishment, including the Charity Organisation Society, which eventually developed close ties with the Mission.

Religous instruction and the conversion of London's outcast population were central to Mrs Ranyard's purposes, as to so many other philanthropists. Though an evangelical, she instructed her missionaries to work with members of all faiths, with the exception of Catholics, whose influence in London alarmed her. For Mrs Ranyard, who embodied the evangelical individualism of the day, the source of social distress was in personal misfortune or moral failing, not the structure of society. This is not to say that she discounted the environment as an influence on character. On the contrary, because the environment did play a part in shaping the lives of the poor, she was determined to improve their domestic and local circumstances through charitable agencies. In her view, the remedy for indigence was to be found in promoting a Christian environment which would transform the poor into accountable, self-respecting members of society. As one of her contemporaries argued, Christianity 'enters the heart and love springs up at its appearing, it enters the house and *peace* is its attendant; wherever it is, whoever it influences, order, self-denial, activity, and benevolence are its attendants'.[10] When delivered with sincerity and kindness, this message, as mentioned earlier, was not without an effect on many poor people, which brought those philanthropic goals of a common culture and social harmony that little bit closer to realization.

The difficulty for Mrs Ranyard and other philanthropists was that so many people lived in such squalor, ignorance and ill-health that expectations of moral reformation and improved family life were premature to say the least. In a Malthusian eyesore like London, visiting could often provide little more than a temporary, patching-up operation. For the large number of the dying attended to by district-visiting societies, ten per cent of the Ranyard Mission's case load, sympathy and a deathbed prayer was often all that could be offered before moving on. A couple of case studies should be sufficient to give an idea of the sort of problems which visitors confronted each day:

> We first went to see a young man who had been crippled and totally helpless for thirteen years from spinal complaint. He lies upon a water bed; every part of him is so paralysed, except in his right hand and arm, that he has no power to move a limb. Nurse helps his mother to move him off his bed twice a week to change the water, and make it fresh for him, but his whole body is so stiffened that it is like lifting a corpse, and any attempt to bend the muscles causes him the greatest agony.[11]

> In visiting a slum in a town in the North of England, our officers entered a hole, unfit to be called a human habitation –

> more like the den of some wild animal – almost the only furniture of which was a filthy iron bedstead, a wooden box to serve for table and chair, while an old tin did duty as a dustbin. The inhabitant of this wretched den was a poor woman, who fled into the darkest corner of the place as our Officer entered. This poor wretch was the victim of a brutal man, who never allowed her to venture outside the door, keeping her alive by the scantiest allowance of food. Her only clothing consisted of a sack tied round her body. Her feet were bare, her hair matted and foul, presenting on the whole such an object as one could scarcely imagine living in a civilized country.[12]

There were innumerable cases such as these which called on benevolent impulses. If they had not been attended to by the charitable, many of them would have been neglected altogether. Confident that what they provided was an effective way of ameliorating human misery, the visiting societies carried on as best they could with available resources. Nineteenth-century poverty and disease were so immediate and overwhelming that abstract debates about the underlying causes of poverty and the value of philanthropy seemed little more than an irrelevance to those on the ground. Unlike social theorists, who had rarely held the hand of a dying child in a hovel, philanthropists had to clean up the mess. They did not always have the time or detachment to question the nature or the ultimate result of their benevolence. Confronted with a scale of pain, dying and death nowadays unimaginable, they were not going to be reasoned out of their humanity by the likes of Harriet Martineau or socialists promising Utopia tomorrow. They could not wait for an overhaul of the social structure or the rise of a welfare state. Many philanthropists encouraged state assistance in such areas as sanitation and housing, but they had to deal with conditions as they were, not as they might be.

For many philanthropic visitors, those well-worn distinctions between 'deserving' and 'undeserving' were often inappropriate too, most notably in the case of abused or ailing children or for those about to die. But it was the serious nature of their work which made visiting societies obsessed with such distinctions. There was never enough money to go around and in the circumstances impostors took on a sinister importance. Begging-letter writers and other ingenious mendicants gave meaning to the term 'deserving poor', a category that respectable people of all classes would have used. Despite the disappointments, abuses, and hypocrisy, visitors from all social backgrounds had reason to be proud of the countless mercies shown to their neighbours. That this work was often so arduous, time-consuming and dangerous to the health of volunteers (many died of disease and some were killed on their rounds) suggests a level of selflessness and commitment which was remarkable. At the level of human contact, in often tragic circumstances, the idea that philanthropy can be reduced to a form of middle-class social control, unresponsive to the genuine grievances of the poor, is not only inadequate but insensitive.

Like many other philanthropic agencies, the Ranyard Mission was alarmed by the physical deterioration in London's slums. Mrs Ranyard had a long-standing interest in health and sanitation. And in touch with nursing programmes in England and Germany, she pioneered the first district nursing programme in London in 1868.[13] Within twenty-five years the Mission had over eighty district nurses, called Bible nurses, working in neighbourhoods across the metropolis. Trained in various London hospitals and given a probationary period in their districts, the Bible nurses were, like their colleagues the Bible women, working class. Supervised by lady volunteers, they carried out duties which blended preventive work, patching up, and religious proselytizing. These duties included referring patients to doctors and local hospitals, inspecting infants in mothers' meetings, and encouraging medical self-help among the poor. This last duty was essential to the scheme, for Mrs Ranyard's medical purpose was to get the poor to nurse themselves. She was very much aware of the degree to which the poor looked after one another in emergencies and hoped to extend and improve these traditions with nursing assistance and advice. Through a programme of medical self-help and religious revival, she hoped to keep families intact and out of pauperism.

A crucial parochial institution in the Victorian campaign for family welfare and spiritual revival was the mothers' meeting.[14] This humble gathering was vital to philanthropic work from the 1850s on, and it remained deeply entrenched in community life until the Second World War. As in the Ranyard Mission, it typically developed out of district-visiting, which had pointed out the need to bring poor women together outside the confines of their homes. This need became all the more urgent to philanthropists when they saw the result of the 1851 religious census, which revealed that church attendance was less than 15 per cent in many poor neighbourhoods. We may dismiss the claim made by her followers that Mrs Ranyard invented the mothers' meeting, for several of them were in operation years before she met her first group of wives and mothers in 1857; but she did more than any other philanthropist to extend its usefulness in London. By 1870, her society alone rented over 230 mission rooms across the metropolis to provide accommodation for its weekly classes. Bible women and Bible nurses joined these meetings, organized by lady superintendents, and turned them into havens of rest, religious education and family welfare.

As a local agency run by women, the mothers' meeting has not much interested historians, but its importance to the philanthropic world and to social improvement was far from negligible. It was, of course, only one of a wide range of parochial charities. It is, however, particularly revealing of the charitable grass roots and takes us deeper into those ideals of parochial service which reached their zenith in the late nineteenth century. With the possible exception of the district-visiting society, the mothers' meeting became the most ubiquitous local agency committed to that philanthropic vision of a reformed society in which the nation's classes were brought into closer contact and greater harmony. No other institution better expresses that most powerful and compelling image of philanthropy – the symbol of charity in art – a mother surrounded by her children. This image served as badge for innumerable charities dedicated to the health and happiness of the British family, but in the mothers' meeting it was life itself. With their infants round them, bowed in needlework, service and prayer, mothers were, to the organizers at least, at one with humanity. To the Victorian mind this was charity incarnate.

With its ingenious mixture of needlework and religion, the mothers' meeting embodied maternal culture. Like paternalists, privileged women believed that society should be organic, pluralistic and hierarchical, led by people of property with a sense of social obligation. But women had their own sources of inspiration, and their parish work drew on a richer seam of compassion and self-sacrifice. In the mothers' meeting, maternalism and the Victorian preoccupation with parochial service, so dependent on the work of women, neatly joined. Cleverly organized, it reached a crucial section of the population, poor wives and mothers, whom philanthropic men were ill-equipped to reach and who were little known to the churches. On average, meetings attracted fifty or sixty regular members, though some of them could boast a weekly attendance of over 300. On the day, usually two hours in the afternoon, members made clothes for their families while receiving religious instruction from the organizers. Stories, lectures and discussions were intermixed with the needlework and prayer. To the members, the meetings offered cheap clothing for the family, a regular diversion from domestic drudgery, a source of female comradeship, a training for children and, for many, the consolation of religion. As with other forms of religious indoctrination, the participants could accept the spiritual message or simply feign respect for it. To the organizers, they were an opportunity for preaching without offending churchmen and a way of helping poor wives and mothers without offending husbands. By encouraging Christianity and its associated familial values, they offered a measure of respectability to local women and children who were often beyond the reach of the churches and other voluntary agencies.

By the 1880s hardly an organization dealing with poor relief was without a mothers' meeting, and along with district nursing it was widely thought to be among the most practical and successful forms of philanthropy. Most women from the higher classes, much heralded for their strong 'parochial sense', would have been under pressure to run one. Most women from the poorer classes would have been invited to join one. The available membership figures, although fragmentary, suggest that in the Edwardian years perhaps as many as a million of them did so each week in Britain, a remarkable figure out of a population of about 12 million women of an age to attend. In Lambeth alone there were fifty-seven meetings run by Anglicans and nonconformists, with 3,600 members.[15] For its part, the Mothers' Union, established by Mrs Mary Sumner in

1876, had around 8,000 branches and 400,000 members in weekly classes at the outbreak of the First World War.[16] Mothers' meetings brought more people together on a regular basis outside the home than any other philanthropic agency. Not even female trade unions could match the membership figures. Despite what some might consider the stumbling block of class differences, contact between the organizers and members often resulted in lasting friendships, as many letters testify.

The success of the mothers' meeting had much to do with its flexibility in responding to local needs. Social, regional and religious differences ensured that the meetings were richly various. A Catholic meeting among Irish mothers in a Liverpool mission would have been a world apart from a meeting of cottage wives in a vicar's library in rural Devon. But wherever they were found, more and more attention was given to a range of social schemes, medical benefits and entertainments as the years went by. Clothing, boot, blanket and coal clubs, savings banks and thrift societies were commonly attached to the meetings in the late nineteenth century. Here the Ranyard Mission, the Ragged School Union and the London City Mission were pioneers. A large meeting in Kilburn boasted a blanket club, a medical club, a doctor's fund, a sick benefit society, a lending library, and a crèche. Others offered a range of entertainments: lantern lectures, reading classes, singing classes and seaside holidays. All had Christmas parties and regular teas. In time, many organizers also turned their meetings to external charitable purposes by the collection of funds and clothing for mission stations and other causes. Marvellously adaptable, they saturated the poor with an ingenious mix of benevolence and self-help. They were so popular that the organizers had to sift through their membership roles to eliminate 'travellers', the mothers' meeting equivalent of today's 'welfare scrounger'.[17]

In addition to its range of social services, the mothers' meeting acted increasingly as a forum for discussion and a clearing house of useful and practical information on family welfare. This function, which Thomas Bernard would have applauded, was especially valuable for the poorest class of mothers, many of whom could not read. From the 1860s, talks on cookery, diet, health and the care of children were common in the meetings. Many of them received advice and material from the COS, the Ladies Sanitary Association (1857) and other central charities. Eventually local government also provided lecturers who went from meeting to meeting. Any issue with domestic implications might be discussed, including venereal disease, votes for women, housing and child abuse. Naturally enough, the issue of children's health came to the fore within mothers' meetings. Growing government concern over child mortality and the needs of national efficiency after the Boer War widened the discussion further. But philanthropists with experience of slum life did not need government statistics on mortality or reports on the physical deterioration of the working classes to make them concerned about children's health. They had noted the dimensions of child mortality and disease on their neighbourhood rounds decades before the state intervened, and had taken action in myriad ways. The mothers' meeting, rooted firmly in the community, was well placed to tackle these problems.

Despite the ubiquity and importance of mothers' meetings, historians have treated the subject of child welfare with virtually no reference to them. Reading many studies of social policy, one gets the impression that the movement to improve the health and conditions of children only got under way with government intervention towards the end of the nineteenth century. The local voluntary institutions which do receive attention are the schools for mothers and infant welfare centres, descendants of the mothers' meeting, which began to appear in the Edwardian years. The reason for their appearance in the histories of child welfare is not simply because of their specialized role in addressing the health of children. It is also because they often qualified for and took up government subsidies and received greater assistance from the male medical establishment; thus they came into the state's purview and consequently the records of government in a way that mothers' meetings did not. Seeing the subject of infant welfare from a male or collectivist perspective, historians of child welfare, like historians of social reform generally, have been prone to overlook parochial voluntary institutions which did not take up state assistance. (Even a great institution with accessible records like the Mothers' Union, which has a long history of lobbying government on social policy, has been neglected.) The very questions they formulate emphasize the role of the government and diminish voluntarism. Mothers' meetings represent a prime example of that Whiggishness in the historiography remarked upon in the Preface, which limits our understanding of philanthropy by its preoccupation with the state.

Causes for the decline of the mothers' meeting can be detected early in the twentieth century, and raise interesting issues. To see the institution as simply a forerunner of government social provision, disappearing with increased state intervention, would be an over-simplification. The range of goods and services on offer in the meetings did become outmoded with changing expectations in regard to the social services and increased state benefits. But reference to the rise of the Welfare State is only a partial explanation of the deterioration of the mothers' meeting. In the broadest sense, anything which threatened family life and material culture endangered it, from birth control to the growth in female employment. The decline in religion and in needlework, and the rising standard of living undercut the original purposes of meetings, turning many of them into little more than occasions for gossip and recreation. The two world wars, whose effects on charity will be discussed in more detail later, dislocated parish life and pressed women into work away from their homes and neighbourhoods. In the increasingly mobile and material world, of altered female perceptions and expectations, the mothers' meeting could not survive intact.

The transfiguration of the mothers' meeting into contemporary Christian women's organizations is a tribute to the institution's resilience and an example of the capacity of voluntary bodies to adapt to changing circumstances. Because of its character, the mothers' meeting did not much enter the late Victorian welfare debate, despite its importance to it. Nor do its descendants attract very much attention. Though it rarely makes the charitable headlines these days, the Mothers' Union remains one of the nation's largest philanthropic bodies. In 1987, it had over 400,000 members in 'women's fellowships', which contribute to the society's extensive activities at home and abroad.[18] The London City Mission, a resilient society which has traditionally worked with deprived groups such as dockers and immigrants, also carries on mothers' meetings in attenuated form. For its part, the Church of England runs 'evangelistic meetings' of young wives, which alternate Bible classes with talks on home-making and child care. Such functions may seem quaint and old fashioned, but their role in community life, not least in fund-raising for good causes, is not inconsiderable. As in the past, many national charities depend on these and other local gatherings of wives and mothers for the supply of clothing, books, toys, and for those innumerable coffee mornings, school fêtes and whist drives which help to pay the bills. They owe a huge debt to Victorian reformers who wove these traditions of parochial service imperceptibly into the life of the community.

IV

Paying the bills

The character of voluntary institutions made fund-raising an obsession. Indeed, it could be argued that philanthropists have shown greater ingenuity in getting money than in spending it. In the nineteenth century, competition for resources was so great that charity organizers missed few opportunities to extract money from the public, from the proverbial 'widow's mite' to the vast sums donated by city companies and the 'charitable ten thousand'. (This latter group was well known to begging-letter writers.) Given their prejudices, the acceptance of money from the state left most nineteenth-century philanthropists feeling decidedly unwell. One authority likened it to the feelings of the curly haired boy in *Nicholas Nickleby*, as his mouth opened before Mrs Squeers's brimstone and treacle spoon.[1] Some charities took their state medicine, but their hesitation to do so, combined with the government's reluctance to offer it, threw philanthropists back on their own resources.

Philanthropic organizers put the public under unrelenting pressure to contribute to charitable causes. It came from the pulpit and the platform, and most directly from the societies themselves. Bishops, MPs and other prominent figures scoured the nation's drawing-rooms for large donations, while unsung volunteers invaded the streets and points of transport to collect small ones, a tradition given a patriotic twist with the arrival of the flag day, which both the Royal National Lifeboat Institution and Alexandra Rose Day (1912) claim to have invented. They also canvassed the general population from door to door. The Bible Society, a charity which did as much to stimulate new fund-raising ideas as any other, had over 10,000 agents, mostly women, operating as household collectors by 1820.[2] Some of them were so assiduous that critics compared them to Excise officers. At the end of the century, the National Society for the Prevention of Cruelty to Children had 6,000 women in the field.[3] Here was the application of district visiting applied to fund-raising, a practice which, though still in use, has given way to direct mail and broadcasting.

Behind the systematic campaign to solicit funds was the assumption that everyone, young and old, rich and poor, was a potential contributor. Millions came from the likes of Thomas Holloway, the patent-medicine vendor, and Angela Burdett-Coutts, whose profession was philanthropy, but no sum was seen as too small to be of service in a good cause. However humble, most people could imagine others more wretched or benighted than themselves. As a washerwoman remarked, 'We ignorant people can indeed pity those who are still more ignorant than we are.'[4] Small contributions from humble subscribers were commonly held to be the most beneficial because they united the nation's aspirations, contributing to a common culture. Regularity and punctuality were guidelines laid down for agents of the societies, and they applied to senior officials on the lookout for legacies to child collectors with their eyes fixed on a penny. When added together, the pounds, shillings and pence came to many millions each year in the nineteenth century. In London alone, charitable receipts came to more than the budgets of several European nations by the 1890s.[5] Widely reported in the press, generosity on such a scale became a source of national pride. If charitable subscriptions were little more than a celebration of property for some citizens, a way of turning privilege into virtue, for most contributors, rich or poor, they were part of a social duty which verged on necessity.

Innovation, audacity, and personal flair have always been hallmarks of charitable money making and never more so than in the nineteenth century. Traditional sources of funds, including the offertory, dinners, balls and concerts carried on as in the eighteenth century with few changes. But new public events were added, such as bazaars, fêtes, and cruises. One invention followed another in the nineteenth century, many of them refinements of the hat and the collection plate. An important one was the collection card, which was widely adopted by the missionary societies in the 1840s and spread to other institutions. Often beautifully engraved, it had space for about twenty subscribers and was passed around among family and friends; when not in use it could be placed on the mantelpiece, a potential rebuke to visitors. The collection box, the direct ancestor of today's colourful charitable containers found in pubs, shops and other public places, appeared at roughly the same time. These attractively labelled wooden boxes, with a slot on the top and a trapdoor underneath, raised phenomenal sums, particularly for foreign missions and medical charities. The Church Missionary Society alone received about £40,000 a year from them by the end of the nineteenth century, and their opening called for small celebrations in communities across the country.[6]

Whether working for a national institution or simply operating as freelance promoters for a local charity, volunteers came up with some highly ingenious schemes, often at some cost to themselves. One ploy, which could be onerous to family and friends, was for the organizer to find ten subscribers, who were to find ten more, each of whom would enlist a fixed number of subscribers. A less elaborate method was simply to pass the plate around at parish mothers' meetings, Sunday schools, entertainments or teas. Enthusiasts like Mrs Gladstone were known to pass it round with the breakfast dishes, which some guests resented, though they paid their share. More imaginatively, the benevolent painted and sold birthday and Christmas cards for various causes, a Victorian tradition which has taken off in the twentieth century. The collection of paper waste for charity began in the 1920s. So too did the use of the wireless, first exploited in 1923 for the Winter Distress League.[7] The charity shop emerged in the early nineteenth century and has become another staple of modern fund-raising. (The British Red Cross alone has 125 of them in operation today across the country.)[8] Originally, shops were the brainchild of philanthropic women who sought a profitable outlet for fancy work made in domestic sewing meetings. They also hawked fancy goods from door to door. It was not unknown for the benevolent to sell their own possessions to pay a charity's tradesmen's bills.

In organization, the use of auxiliaries or associated branches, so important to charities today, was the greatest fund-raising innovation in the nineteenth century. Pioneered by the missionary and

Bible societies, virtually every institution which sought national support adopted the system by the 1840s. Once established, branches typically contributed more than half of the income of their respective societies. They were tendrils of organized benevolence, shooting across the country in search of local sustenance. They were a clever way of bringing parochial service to bear on national causes. Agents travelled around the country to assist local residents in setting them up, and they paid particular attention to women and children, and to specific occupational groups such as mechanics or seamen. Many branches operated through Sunday schools or Bible classes attached to churches, chapels, or factories. Others grew out of domestic meetings of women. But anyone with the time and enthusiasm was free to recruit others, though if the cause was out of tune with local opinion it was unlikely to succeed. Often with elaborate constitutional arrangements, branches conformed to rules coming out of headquarters, though they had sufficient autonomy to encourage local initiative. Run by committees and made up of members who subscribed a certain sum, their essential purpose was to raise money. The mix of organizational skill and individual flair with which this was accomplished may be seen in the accounts of the societies themselves. The Bible Society canvassed the country from door to door, but it also boasted of a working woman in Dorset who trained her parrot to say to visitors, 'Put something in the Bible box'. It collected £10 before it flew away.[9]

Women and children became the backbone of the auxiliary movement, despite some initial misgivings about using their offices in the early nineteenth century. Like mothers' meetings, visiting societies and other parish organizations, the work of a neighbourhood branch of a prominent charity contributed to a heightened sense of the local community's role in national affairs, while it provided skills in administration and a diversion from household routine for the participants. Respectable entertainments were an integral part of the life of these charitable associations. They were especially important to children in religious communities cut off from the centres of culture and where restrictions on entertainments were often considerable. Whether going to hear a missionary back from Africa with a regenerated heathen at his side, or playing at shopping in a children's bazaar for the local branch of a charitable society, such diversions combined duty and recreation in a manner suited to the moral sensibilities of the day. This compelling mix of benevolence and entertainment is so deeply rooted in British community life that it largely goes unnoticed, and is often taken for granted even by those charities which are its beneficiaries.

Children's charitable activity flowed initially from the enthusiasm of parents, particularly evangelical mothers, who saw the early inculcation of benevolence in their children as a religious and social duty. Good works were a hopeful sign that a child was ready for conversion, which was all the more urgent in a time of high child mortality. Charities took advantage of this domestic indoctrination and organized children for their own financial purposes and with the view of bringing up future generations of subscribers. The earliest children's associations, with their own rules and committees, emerged in the early nineteenth century in connection with the missionary movement. The Bible Society and the Church Missionary Society, among others, soon discovered that the young made ideal collectors, for parents and neighbours did not like to look ungenerous in the eyes of children working for charity. Many societies hired specialists to work with children's groups, which were given distinctive names. In the RSPCA they were 'Bands of Mercy', in the Ranyard Mission 'Little Helpers'. Most of the societies which adopted children's branches became increasingly dependent on them for revenue. As children invariably carried out their fund-raising duties in the immediate neighbourhood, this was yet another inducement to taking local voluntary action seriously. The Methodist Missionary Society, which had a large following among the working classes, raised over £1 million from juvenile missionary associations in the nineteenth century, and their annual reports show that by 1900 about 20 per cent of their receipts came from children's collections. By then, women and children altogether contributed roughly 70 per cent of that charity's income.[10]

In the Victorian years there was a rapid advance in children's organizations and associated fund-raising ideas which increased charitable revenues. The missionary and Bible societies were among the most assiduous, as the success of the Methodists suggests. They published an assortment of children's periodicals, dispatched lecturers to Sunday schools, set up libraries and museums for children, organized summer gatherings, and as a climax to their activities arranged great annual events at Exeter Hall and elsewhere. But other charities were not far behind in paying more and more attention to the philanthropic impulses of children. (As some have argued, they turned them into mechanical, unfeeling gestures.) Bands of Hope kept the young in touch with the evils of drink; the League of Pity, founded in 1894 by the NSPCC, brought them into the campaign against child abuse; and the Children's Union of the Waifs and Strays Society (1881) kept them in touch with the poor. Many of these organizations are still in operation and continue to provide an invaluable source of funds to their respective societies. The NSPCC, for example, raised nearly £300,000 in 1979 from 'spell ins'.[11] There is hardly a primary or Sunday school in Britain today which, by one means or another, does not send money to the coffers of national charities. A careful analysis of the revenues of a wide range of contemporary institutions, including the RSPCA, Dr Barnardo's and the Church of England Children's Society (1881) would confirm that there has been no let-up in the use of the young in fund-raising.

If children's charitable activity provided a valuable source of funds to particular societies, the subscriptions and legacies of women were crucial to many others. Beginning in the early nineteenth century, there was a rapid growth of societies managed by women which depended almost entirely on female support. But institutions run by men also became increasingly indebted to the female purse. In the missionary, tract and Bible societies, the percentages of female subscriptions rose to around 50 per cent during the century. In the RSPCA female contributions were higher still, rising to about 70 per cent by 1900. (The RSPCA only admitted women to its General Council in 1896.) Women showed less interest in distressed foreigners and the ruptured poor, but generously funded most societies which related to female experience. Among their favoured causes were moral reform, temperance, anti-slavery, refuges and reformatories, and any institution dealing with children or the protection of female servants. In the Governesses' Benevolent Institution (1841) they provided over 60 per cent of the funds; in the Institution for the Employment of Needlewomen (1860) about 75 per cent. In the Ranyard Mission, which had a mixed management of men and women, female subscriptions made up about 80 per cent of the total. But these figures, while impressive in themselves, do not begin to suggest the ingenuity of women in raising money from others. The perfunctory 'thank you to women volunteers', common in the annual reports, disguises just how marvellously effective women could be in a time of rising costs. The feminization of organized philanthropy began with the generosity of women and their genius for fund-raising.[12]

That much maligned institution, the bazaar, was the most pervasive female method of raising money for charity in Victorian Britain.[13] That bazaars continue to be held each year in communities across the country, not least in schools and churches, is a tribute to their flexibility. Making an appearance in the second decade of the nineteenth century, they became fashionable in the 1830s when the Queen and other members of the Royal family turned up as stallholders at the grandest of them. Synonymous with women's philanthropic work, bazaars soon became part of the social fabric, bringing together the fairground and commerce, or entertainment coupled with a sense of gain. Many in the charitable establishment have taken the bazaar for granted, perhaps because it was a female invention, yet it has been probably the most profitable public event ever devised in the history of philanthropy. (The charity concert may surpass it someday with its use of TV satellites and rock music.) Bazaars, ladies' sales, or fancy fairs as they were variously called, raised tens of millions of pounds in the nineteenth century alone. Most of this money came from small local sales held in school-rooms, church halls or out of doors in the vicarage garden or an open field. Vast numbers of them were held annually, usually in the summer or at Christmas, for the auxiliaries of the great charities; others were organized whenever merited by a local cause, such as the redecoration of the vicarage or the enlargement of a school. Every conceivable cause was supported, from promoting working-men's clubs to funding militant Suffragettes. More recently they have been used to aid Maoists in China and to re-elect Mrs Thatcher.

Because it is so commonplace, a part of virtually everyone's social experience, the bazaar is a most revealing institution. For women, it offered an opportunity for public service that was compatible with household routine; it gave them opportunities for friendly rivalry and display; and it legitimized trade and manual work from which middle-class women at least were excluded. It was, moreover, an expression of their coming of age in philanthropic causes, a reflection of that compassion which was thought to be at the heart of female character. For children, it broke the school routine, provided recreation and opportunities for self-expression. It also brought the community together, not least in the making of elaborate preparations. In most bazaars there was a happy mixture of the classes, which working for charitable purposes encouraged generally. As patrons or stallholders, local worthies, and sometimes distinguished outsiders, joined in that spirit of the occasion and plied their wares among the populace. In the bazaar we can see people of all ages and social classes in that most human of pursuits, buying and selling. Here they found bargains which added to the clutter of their drawing-rooms, made contacts, passed an idle hour, and all the while took satisfaction from the performance of a duty. Few other forms of philanthropy are so well suited to human behaviour, which is why it has adapted so well to contemporary life.

The bazaar was typically a local affair, but its flexibility was such that it could be turned to great purposes. Most bazaars in Victorian Britain made sums of less than £100, but the grand fancy fairs could make many thousands. The Voluntary hospitals especially owed a huge debt to them. The London Hospital received £10,000 from one in 1898, a sizeable sum which helped to keep the institution free from bankruptcy and ministerial control. But the largest bazaar in the nineteenth century was that in aid of the Anti-Corn Law League, held in Covent Garden Theatre, which raised £25,000 in May 1845 over seventeen days. It was part trade fair, part amusement, part politics, a tribute to free trade and a preview of the Great Exhibition. As one delirious free trader put it, it turned 'a commonplace thing – often a mart for children's trumpery' into 'a great and holy thing'.[14] The preparations for it drew on the industry of every class in British life. An interesting element in the preparations was the use of volunteers who canvassed Manchester and other cities for contributions. Here again, we see the use of district visiting applied to another charitable purpose and the local initiative that impressed itself even on national events.

Bazaars and the many other charitable fund-raising ideas kept many a society afloat. However profitable, they rarely provided income sufficient to satisfy the many sanguine philanthropists who were obsessed with growth. Confident of public support, they even pursued schemes which, on the face of it, compromised first principles. The Royal National Lifeboat Institution, for example, accepted a state grant to help it survive a financial crisis in 1854. (It opted to become fully independent again fifteen years later.)[15] Despite their reservations, increasing numbers of charitable societies turned to the state, especially in areas where philanthropy took on board more than it could cope with alone, or where government legislation was necessary to complement charitable aims. Philanthropists recognized that government action was necessary to conquer slavery or to counteract the distresses created by factory conditions. Was there not scope for government to finance charitable projects in other areas such as education and the protection of children, while leaving philanthropists in charge?

As the nineteenth century progressed, a typically British compromise between philanthropists and the state developed, which set a pattern of relations between government and the voluntary sector. In education, a field pioneered by philanthropy, the state voted building grants to the National Society and the British and Foreign School Society in 1833. The charities determined the conditions on which the state, with some timidity, contributed. In accepting their junior status in the partnership, the government left the societies free to carry on their denominational rivalries for decades, and this contributed to the delay in bringing in a state system of education. Criminal and vagrant children were other targets of joint effort. In reformatories and other institutions set up by private individuals for juvenile delinquents, there developed an unlikely but not unsuccessful partnership with the state following the Youthful Offenders Act of 1854. Despite the grants, which could be more than half of their income, and inspection which state certification entailed, these institutions nevertheless retained their essential independence. Industrial schools, which sought to teach vagrant children rudimentary skills and the habits of honest industry, were taken up by the state in a similar fashion in the mid-Victorian years, without undermining their character as independent, voluntary institutions.[16]

The acceptance of public money by philanthropists did not unsettle the Victorian belief in the primacy of charity over state action. For their part, nineteenth-century governments did not wish to challenge this belief, even as grants to selected charities grew larger. Before the 1880s, few people dissented from the view that the state's role in welfare policy should be strictly limited to a responsibility for those undeserving cases administered by the poor law. In Victorian Britain the larger share of the welfare bill continued to be picked up by individuals, not as taxpayers, but as fellow citizens and human beings. To those of a philanthropic disposition, the state was thought to be too bureaucratic, impersonal and unwieldy to tackle social ills which required individual discretion. Unfettered voluntary action, it was argued, was beneficial to all parties, not least the donors, who in choosing between the objects of their benevolence received a moral training and lessons in self-discipline. Such views were natural enough given the liberal ethos that social evils flowed from personal misfortune or individual inadequacy rather than from faults in the structure of society. They were certainly convenient for Treasury officials, whose admiration for individual accountability went hand in hand with a passion for retrenchment.

V

Challenges and adaptation

In a society so conducive to voluntary effort as Victorian Britain, it could be said that philanthropists were their own worst enemies. Charities had the unhappy tendency to fall out of repair or into dispute. Relations between charitable institutions were often little short of chaotic. Across the country confusion and muddle proliferated. In the 1870s, for example, there were five national charities campaigning 'to reduce Sunday gloom'.[1] The atmosphere of sectarian rivalry and petty jealousy, self-interest and dislike of London rule, angered charitable critics and worried sympathizers. As the historian J. R. Green complained, there were 'hundreds of agencies at work over the same ground without concert or co-operation or the slightest information as to each other's exertions.'[2] In parts of London, four or five competing district-visiting societies besieged poor households each week. This was not only an invasion of privacy and a threat to individual liberty, said the critics, but an invitation to hypocrisy and improvidence. In such circumstances, hostility to philanthropists and exploitation of their good offices thrived. As a Yorkshire beggar told a district visitor when asked if he could read or write: 'No Ma'am, I can't . . . and if I'd known as much when I was a child as I do now, I'd never have learnt to walk or talk.'[3] Such remarks alarmed Victorians addicted to social science.

Attempts to organize and rationalize the resources of voluntary societies were longstanding, but in the late nineteenth century ever more urgent. Rising contributions raised expectations of their successful application. Moreover, the persistence of poverty was an acute embarrassment in a society of obvious wealth which prided itself on social improvement. It is impossible to identify the origin of the idea of philanthropic organization, but a list of coordinating charities would include the Metropolitan Visiting and Relief Association (1843), the Society for the Relief of Distress (1860), the Liverpool Central Relief Society (1863), the COS (1869), and the National Council of Social Service (1919), now the National Council for Voluntary Organisations. Some coordinating charities participated in grandiose schemes, but most saw clearly that small local organizations were crucial to their work. Placing a premium on neighbourliness and the sanctity of family life, which were the essence of informal and local benevolence, they supported innumerable visiting, provident, and self-help schemes.

An important element in the makeup of the organizing charities was their belief that science could and should be applied to personal service. They took to social statistics when they became the rage in the mid-Victorian years with a naïve enthusiasm born of former factual deprivation. Self-help was to be invigorated by social casework, Christian kindness was to be tempered by statistical investigation. What they brought to customary practice was greater system and principles of political economy. The hoped-for revolutionary improvement in the condition of the poor did not take place, but in other respects the results were deemed satisfactory. Under the direction of Charles Loch, assisted by social workers like Octavia Hill and Bernard Bosanquet, the COS took the lead. The organizing societies reduced indiscriminate alms-giving, provided more professional training to generations of charitable workers, and further coordinated the work of voluntary bodies and statutory authorities. By grafting social science methods on to religious precept and parochial organization, they encouraged more sophisticated approaches to the problems of poor relief.

It was unfortunate for the advocates of philanthropy that just as they felt that they were putting their own house in order, assumptions about the causes of poverty were shifting and the government began to take a greater interest in social matters. In time, social statistics, so beloved by the more progressive voluntarists, would provide the government with the information necessary to take over a larger share of erstwhile charitable responsibility. Philanthropists had promoted an understanding with the statutory authorities, advantageous to themselves, that individual reformation was their concern. But toward the end of the nineteenth century this formula, which was part of a pre-industrial (and perhaps also of a post-industrial?) outlook was beginning to be seen as outdated in view of social realities. Despite philanthropy's ever-rising revenues and greater coordination, an intolerable level of poverty persisted, while the idealized 'scientific' cooperation with government never lived up to expectations. Government itself was being drawn into the welfare debate by its assistance to charitable societies, its social investigations, and its intervention in such matters as sanitation and factory life. Suspicions grew that private charity was unable to cope with the central issue of poverty. Descriptions of urban deprivation such as *The Bitter Cry of Outcast London* (1883) by the Revd Andrew Mearns added to the suspicions, while reminding the rich of their social obligations.

Sensational reports about social conditions, which philanthropists often penned themselves, made people more sensitive to the growing body of data on the conditions of life of the lower classes which was coming into circulation. In particular, Charles Booth's dispassionate inquiry, *The Life and Labour of the People in London*, published in stages between 1889–1903, and the philanthropist Seebohm Rowntree's *Poverty: A Study of Town Life* (1901), added ammunition to those who were coming to different conclusions about the causes of poverty and the best way to remedy it. Notable among these social theorists was, of course, Beatrice Webb, whose Minority Report of the Royal Commission on the Poor Laws (1905–9) recommended a more positive government response to poverty and unemployment. In Mrs Webb's 'Heavenly City' of Fabian socialism, social problems required something more comprehensive that what was on offer from competing charitable bodies dependent on volunteers, or the social philosophy of the COS with its inducements to self-help. Unlike philanthropists, who flourished in diversity, she sought unity in social life. In her view, the causes of destitution were to be found in the structure of society, not in individual or familial circumstances. What was needed was a radical overhaul of the social services and the promotion of a national minimum. She did not deny the need for voluntary bodies, but the community at large, not individuals and communities in isolation, must be the driving force in improving the British standard of life.

Against this background of opinion and the pioneering, albeit piecemeal, Liberal social legislation of 1905–11, philanthropy found its status diminished in the welfare field. As one authority remarked, 'When the focus shifted from "the Poor" and what could be done to relieve their distress, to poverty and what could be done to abolish it, then it became inevitable that the State should intervene more decisively and that the scope of private charity should be correspondingly altered.'[4] The belief that poverty could be 'abolished' presupposed an understanding of what caused it in the first place. Here philanthropists, fragmented by their respective campaigns and conditioned by the Christian view that poverty was ineradicable, were at a disadvantage in the changing climate of opinion. Pulling in different directions, they were not well suited to an investigation of the relationship between poverty, old age and unemployment which came into fashion in the late nineteenth century. Many of philanthropy's collectivist critics, on the other hand, by a sleight of mind, assumed that their more sophisticated appreciation of the causes of poverty, made possible by social statistics, would lead to its elimination. All that was needed was the will of government and the right financial arrangements. In their writings they helped to create the illusion that the state could transform society, as if by magic. They took it for granted that the poor themselves wished for an extension of statutory provision and that taxpayers would happily pay for it. The expectations thus aroused would place an enormous burden on later governments and form an ineradicable part of the prevailing climate of opinion in late twentieth-century Britain.

To those for whom the state held out the promise of social progress, whether collectivist or not, philanthropy was not only insufficient, but still too often ignorant and patronizing. (That charities traditionally worked within the existing social structure made them anathema to many socialists, who assumed that in accepting social divisions philanthropists approved of them.) To many people, parochial service, despite its opportunities to create personal bonds between volunteers and the deprived, was too closely identified with religious zeal. It was of little consequence to those who saw social problems in political terms, requiring political solutions. As Brian Harrison has noted, the pioneers of state aid, from Edwin Chadwick to William Beveridge, did not much identify personally with those they sought to relieve. Though a Sub-Warden at Toynbee Hall as a young man, Beveridge distrusted 'the saving power of culture and of missions and of isolated good feelings'.[5] For her part, Beatrice Webb remarked that ' "A million sick" have always seemed actually more worthy of self-sacrificing devotion than the "child sick in a fever", preferred by Mrs Browning's *Aurora Leigh*'.[6] This impersonal approach to welfare, the belief in the efficacy of legislation, state intervention and large centralized bureaucracies was to become as compelling a remedy for social ills to its advocates in the mid-twentieth century as individual service was to the Victorians. What they inherited from the nineteenth century was a paternalism, which exceeded that of the philanthropists they often disavowed.

The philanthropist Josephine Butler argued in 1869 that large legislative welfare systems were 'masculine' in character, while the parochial system of personal ministration, with its corollary of recreating domestic life in institutions, was essentially 'feminine'.[7] The fact that Beatrice Webb was a leading advocate of a system of state-based welfare illustrates the limitations of such a generality, but the distinction pervades the literature. Poor law officials, who dealt with the paupers wholesale, were often unsympathetic to women visitors who wished to minister to individuals. To Home Office officials responsible for the prison service after 1877, the notion of treating prisoners as part of an extended family was both alien and unmanly; by the end of the century they curtailed the operations of women visitors. Political economists too complained of amateurish and sentimental female philanthropists, whose charities were largely pragmatic solutions to immediate problems. In turn, female philanthropists were quick to criticize government bureaucracy as inflexible and inhuman. And they sometimes spoke of the irrelevance of political economy to life as lived in poor neighbourhoods. Abstract debates about the value of social service and distinctions between the deserving and undeserving did not mean so much to women, whose training was typically unanalytical and domestic. On their neighbourhood rounds, they were confronted with a scale of human misery that impaired detachment. One woman, writing of the Salvation Army's experience, remarked in 1906 that 'the real work of social reform . . . appears to be so far beneath the notice of Parliament, municipal authorities, and Poor Law Guardians'.[8]

It is worth asking whether the growing authority of women in charity predisposed male planners to favour programmes that were relatively free from female interference or control. Large bureaucracies created by legislation and paid for out of tax did not require such immediate accountability as charities paid for out of subscriptions. Perhaps the evolution of the state welfare services, created and dominated by men, was not unaffected by the feminization of philanthropy which took place in the nineteenth century. (In addition to female financial power, it was estimated in the 1890s that half a million women volunteers worked full time in charity and another 20,000 were paid officials in philanthropic societies.)[9] Male officials in departments of government, especially central government, were protected from strong-minded women and their tendency to see social problems in moral and parochial terms. 'Masculine officialism', to use the words of one leading female philanthropist, had been an obstacle to the progress of women in organized philanthropy; it broke down through their sheer hard work and the persuasiveness of the purse. It was to rear its head again in the departments of state, where it has proved, if anything, a greater obstacle to women. This has reinforced their enthusiasm for voluntary action.

State social action began to pose a challenge to charitable predominance in the Edwardian years, but the First World War was much more unsettling to philanthropists. Most of them were zealous in support of the war effort; and many of them demonstrated their patriotism by promoting the sale of war bonds, assisting recruitment drives and caring for the casualties. They did not at first recognize the danger war posed to the way of life of their communities. The sheer scale and horror of the carnage dealt a blow to religious faith and encouraged men and women to look elsewhere for consolation. As men went to the front, parish life was fractured. As women took their place in agriculture and industry they had less time to give to those institutions which might otherwise have filled their idle hours. An agent of the Ragged School Union put it neatly in 1916: women and girls were 'cast from the service of the home and class amid the whirl of wheels.[10] The growing difficulty of recruiting younger men and women to parish charities meant that older members had to carry on as best they could for as long as they could. In the changing social terrain, men and women who had travelled far from home in wartime, who had taken up new employments and seen new possibilities, did not always wish to return to the disrupted rituals and institutions of parish life. Many did not return at all. With ever more distractions and rival centres of loyalty, charitable institutions, especially religious ones, had to adapt or die.

A less dramatic challenge to Christian charity, which would have profound implications for familial and parochial traditions, was taking place in the early decades of the twentieth century in the form of changes in medical practice. Much attention has been given to Darwinism in the decline of Christianity, but chloroform and chemotherapy were probably more important to it. As medical treatment improved with the introduction of new drugs and painkillers, Christianity lost some of its transforming power. Souls slipped away as more could be done to save bodies. The Ranyard nurses, for example, struggled to sustain their religious enthusiasm in a time when medicine and religion were becoming uneasy partners. As their nursing practices became more scientific and beneficial, their religion became diffused; they adapted by giving assistance to the Girl Guides (1910) and running recreation centres for the elderly. (Only in 1965 were they incorporated into the Health Services.) Lying-in and maternity charities, which were a feature of Victorian communities, declined with the greater use of hospital care by expectant mothers. The separation of the living from the dying, which became more common as sick and terminal patients were removed from their homes into hospitals and institutions, broke the cycle of domestic Christianity and reduced the number of those ritual visits of family and neighbours around the domestic sick-bed. Whether patients preferred the quick, concentrated medical service in hospitals to the greater degree of personal contact they got from charitable visitors and family at home is questionable. The current popularity of out-patient care and home births suggests that the public today think that something is missing in the services provided inside institutions.

As religion declined during the twentieth century the individualist opposition to state intervention probably diminished. Arguably, the growth of government responsibility for welfare contributed to the devitalization of Christian charity and by implication Christianity itself. (Did a decline in charitable tithes make a social tax more urgent?) As the state's activity in the social sphere tended to divorce material from spiritual welfare, philanthropy became more a question of personal choice. Many Christians, of course, continued to support church and chapel charities and the foreign and city missions, many of which have soldiered on in what might be thought to be an unfavourable climate. (Today, there is a tendency to overlook their work, in part because they value their individuality and rarely join coordinating bodies like the National Council for Voluntary Organisations.) For those of a philanthropic disposition who were losing faith, allegiances often shifted from religious charities with traditional pieties and values to other agencies thought to be more relevant to social need and in tune with changing attitudes. Here they would come into communion with philanthropy's temporal wing.

Philanthropy found new life by a shift of emphasis to contemporary social issues, where the atmosphere was increasingly free of sectarian overtones. Most dramatically, the First World War offered fresh fields for voluntary social action. It contributed to a loss of faith and disrupted parish charity, but it enlarged the need for personal service and national effort. The vast amount of war-related work undertaken by new organizations like the Women's Institutes, founded in 1915 to assist in food production, the King George's Fund for Sailors (1917), the National Council for One Parent Families (1918) and the Royal British Legion (1921) are testimony to the willingness of philanthropists to take on the challenge. It was often met with the blessing of the state. There was formal co-operation too, which underlined the growing secularization of many philanthropic bodies. Charities for the relief of families of soldiers and sailors, for example, worked with the Local Government Board, and the National Federation of Women's Institutes received grants from a department of the Board of Agriculture, though it eventually gave them up. Unemployment in the 1930s provided another opportunity for voluntary action, and it resulted in the creation of a wide range of charitable agencies outside the churches (those still inside were no less active), which served as repositories of moral values. They carried forward a tradition dominated by religious charities in the nineteenth century. As volunteers joined philanthropy's temporal wing, the idea of parochial service with its traditional religious associations was being transformed gradually into secularized community service. It often implied a community wider than the parish or neighbourhood.

War-related charity reminds us, if reminding is needed, that just as government was taking greater initiative in social policy, various philanthropic institutions were being formed. The list of prominent national charities established early in this century is impressive. As well as those already mentioned, it includes the Imperial Cancer Research Fund (1902), the National Art Collections Fund (1903), the Scout Association (1908), the Carnegie United Kingdom Trust (1913), Save the Children Fund (1919), the Wellcome Foundation (1924), the National Union of Townswomen's Guilds (1929), which grew out of the women's suffrage movement, the Pilgrim Trust (1930), the Youth Hostels Association (1930) and the King George's Jubilee Trust (1935). We should not lose sight of the continuing importance of community-based charities in these years, but national institutions tended to greater and greater size. The emergence of large charitable trusts and foundations, whose commissions allowed them to deal with a wide range of issues, was to become a feature of twentieth-century British philanthropy. The model for them came from America, as did much of the money.

The trend to bigger institutions in the twentieth century was in part shaped by the criticism that charities in the past were too small in scale to be effective and too unstable and understaffed to provide adequate care. Perhaps the model of government bureaucracy also encouraged largeness of scale, especially to those foundations which worked with departments of state. (It is noticeable that the institutions created by men were more centralized than those established by women, where the numerous branches were typically self-governing.) The size of many charities meant that appeals to the public had to be broad, thus they tended to play down religious associations and doctrinal differences. The larger the institution the more likely it was to distance individual philanthropists from beneficiaries. This posed a threat to personal service, which was all the more evident in those philanthropic bodies which worked with government agencies where utility and cost-efficiency were at a premium.

In the inter-war years there were various schemes to coordinate public and private welfare programmes, often brought about by the intolerable levels of unemployment. The Majority Report of the Royal Commission on the Poor Laws had recommended closer cooperation and the First World War had shown its usefulness in certain areas. Coordinating charities like the Liverpool Council of Voluntary Aid (1909) and the National Council of Social Service were in tune with the promptings of the Poor Law Report and took the lead in bringing together charitable and statutory bodies. They represented a compromise between voluntary and state provision by which rigid choices between them were avoided. Against the background of the changing nature of social problems this had advantages. But even with the best intentions, the coordination of services was bound to be problematic because of conflicting priorities and the *ad hoc* character of both government legislation and charitable activity. As the National Council of Social Service discovered, bureaucratic constraints and doctrinal differences hindered the development of closer relations between charities as well as between charities and government. In the relief of unemployment, as elsewhere, religious groups preferred to act in isolation. Some Labour councils thought volunteers were doing jobs that should be done by paid employees. While there was no necessary contradiction in their aims, disagreements between Socialists and philanthropists, who were often Liberals, Tories or simply traditionalists, caused strains.

Despite differences of opinion, large numbers of people responded to charitable appeals to combat unemployment in the inter-war years. (Tellingly, the creation of the Unemployment Assistance Board in 1934, which established a large staff of government social workers, did not spell the end of the visiting societies.) As in the past, working through communities down to the afflicted families was the priority. The then Prince of Wales, Patron of the National Council of Social Service, clearly understood this. When he addressed the issue of unemployment in a speech in the Albert Hall in early 1932, he called on the good neighbour to break the problem 'into little pieces'. Within the year individuals or voluntary groups had initiated 2,300 projects, including visiting schemes, clubs, settlements and workshops, some of them started by the unemployed themselves, which catered to well over a million people. Such a response suggested that those familiar remedies of personal service and self-help espoused by the Victorians still had a great attraction. When the Ministry of Labour under the national government agreed to make grants available to some of these schemes through the National Council of Social Service, the Left denounced the decision as a cheap and devious way of buying off the unemployed.[11]

Despite the emergence of many new societies and foundations and the generous response of the public to continual appeals, many philanthropists, long on the defensive over health and welfare issues, began to lose confidence in the inter-war years. Some voluntarists, most notably those dealing in family planning and infant welfare, accepted their limitations and welcomed increased government funding and control. Those who wished to keep the government at bay, or sought to dish the socialists, had the never-ending task of scratching around for private money in a depressed economy. This was a special burden to older institutions, such as the voluntary hospitals, where operating costs were high and getting higher. Uncertainty narrowed priorities and called for ever greater rationalization, which drained public confidence. But in the new political democracy between the wars expectations of social life were rising. The state of the voluntary hospitals, the relief of unemployment, and child welfare attracted attention. Increasingly, these issues suggested a need for new forms of administration and a greater role for the government. Those philanthropists alarmed by their altered circumstances and the ill-defined relationship of charity and the state could immure themselves in the past or look to what they thought to be the future.

The charitable world had contained formidable figures such as Charles Loch and Octavia Hill of the COS and General William Booth of the Salvation Army at the turn of the century, but between the wars it was short of prominent leaders and fresh ideas. One of the reasons for this was probably that many potential recruits to voluntarism, particularly men, were swept up in the tide of parliamentary and municipal affairs which had been expanding at such a rapid rate in the early years of the century. After the First World War and the rise of Labour, the state, not philanthropy, must have appeared the wave of the future to many of them, to some a better choice of career. In the voluntary world, a significant minority, represented by the Councils of Social Service, had spearheaded the campaign to forge a more professional and effective partnership with the state. They found an ally in Elizabeth Macadam, a leading social worker, who believed a pact with government was both necessary and desirable. By 1934, when she published *The New Philanthropy*, she had accepted the predominant role of the state in the social services and the need to mobilize voluntary action under government control. The expression of such opinions would have put Charles Loch and Octavia Hill into a voluntary hospital. Nevertheless, Macadam's committed views have been taken as representive of the inter-war philanthropy. They were not, but they anticipated post-war developments.

The 'new philanthropy' of the 1930s, in so far as it existed, was synonymous with state partnership. It had an underlying materialistic ethos which further narrowed discussions of voluntary activity to the relief of poverty. Macadam, among others, was so enamoured of the possibilities of partnership that she was blind to the vast amount of charitable work dealing with poor relief which operated without any reference to the state at all. One wonders what parochial charities, which prided themselves on their autonomy, would have made to her delight in bureaucratic supervision and regulation? Her belief that welfare charities were 'invariably linked in some way or other with the all embracing activities of central or local government' was wishful thinking and contrary to her own evidence.[12] Given her readiness to see voluntary bodies forgo some of their independence, she did not appreciate the resilience of those societies which protected their freedom by shifting their functions into areas where partnership was unnecessary. 'Sporadic charity' which emerged in response to disaster or personal appeals made her unhappy, for it was inefficient and uncontrolled; she preferred the rigid budgeting of the public social services, perhaps forgetting that charity had benefits for the benevolent as well as the beneficiary. The 'new philanthropy' was a hybrid. It reconciled the statism of the Webbs with the 'scientific charity' of the COS. Designed with social workers in mind, it was so attenuated that many Victorians would hardly recognize it as philanthropy at all. It was not immune from red tape and a partnership with government given to fitful relations. It took the outbreak of war to bring it into prominence.

The Second World War's impact on state social policy has attracted such attention that its impact on charitable activity has been obscured. As in 1914, domestic and international crisis both threatened and challenged voluntarists; and it accelerated their work with state officials. At the local level the picture is very confusing, for while all communities and their institutions were affected, some were more affected than others, depending on the degree of bomb damage and whether there was an influx of evacuees, troops or war workers.[13] In general, the war disrupted the work of most charities, killed off others, and promoted a host of new ones. The process of decline and renewal reveals the tenacity of charitable impulses. Many societies suffered bomb damage, including thirty-eight of the missions of the Ragged School Union.[14] But out of the ashes other voluntary bodies emerged, such as the Bombed Sites Producers Association, which turned derelict land into allotments. Other volunteers turned rooms let by charities for mothers' meetings and evening classes into recreation centres for servicemen or wards for casualties of the Blitz. A major problem for many societies was how to cope with the continual calling up of their volunteers for the forces. The answer was for women to fill many of the places formerly held by men, which further strengthened their already powerful position within the voluntary world. More often than not, it was to women that communities or the government looked during the war for the development of new organizations and the unsung labour which kept them in operation.

Some of the new charities came and went with the war. The 'Bundles for Britain' campaign, for example, provided American money and supplies for the voluntary hospitals during the Blitz.[15] Other projects had more enduring responsibilities, such as the Women's Voluntary Service, set up with government assistance in

1938, and the Association of Jewish Refugees in Great Britain (1940). The emergency also gave important work to established charities; the British Red Cross and the Order of St John of Jerusalem (1888) ran the auxiliary hospitals on behalf of the Ministry of Health. In the evacuation of children, various societies assisted Whitehall by taking care of reception arrangements. Others provided volunteers for air raid precautions. The Citizens' Advice Bureaux (1938) dealt with an estimated ten million inquiries during the war. Like other societies, it received substantial funds from the state, which raised the question about its independence. The WVS became auxiliary to over twenty government departments. Here was a hybrid body worthy of Macadam's 'new philanthropy', which saw volunteers essentially as helpmeets of the state. The use of female volunteers under the direction of male officialdom, which had been a feature within philanthropy, now became entrenched in philanthropy's partnership with government. This helps to explain why many charities felt that they were being taken for granted by the state, and some still do.

In the atmosphere of 'total war', with the government making inroads on every front, the voluntary world was bound to look diminished even where it thrived. In creating the exposing scarcity and deprivation, the war made traditional philanthropic remedies look all the more inadequate. Compared to the prospect of universal state provision offered by the Beveridge Report, published in 1942, the charitable emphasis on local initiative was not very compelling, nor were appeals to self-help after all the sacrifice the war itself demanded. With the vast expansion of the post-war social services, voluntarists with a welfare role had to take stock. Far fewer cashed it in than is sometimes imagined. Government absorbed many of philanthropy's health and welfare functions, but most institutions soldiered on, as did neighbours and families. Various local societies, many of them still church or chapel based, had a welfare role peripheral to government concerns. Many others transformed into new institutions with a stronger social element in their makeup, accelerating a process which was under way before the war. The 350,000 members of the National Federation of Women's Institutes carried on their social work with little interruption, but in peacetime gave greater emphasis to educational programmes and to bringing together country women in social activities. The Women's Voluntary Service, with 900,000 members (only 200 paid staff) in 1948, continued to offer a wide range of social services at the behest of government, services which the state could not provide. So did the Citizens' Advice movement, for hundreds of autonomous local bureaux, linked to the National Council of Social Service, were to play an important part in post-war reconstruction.[16]

Some of the more prominent national charities, mirroring local institutions, shifted their priorities. A few changed their names. The COS became the Family Welfare Association in 1946, a label which more accurately reflected its chief concern by this time, family casework. In response to the creation of the National Health Service, from the beginning heavily dependent on voluntary effort, the formidable King Edward's Hospital Fund for London (1897) pioneered fresh initiatives and prospered. The Oxford Committee for Famine Relief (1942), which became simply Oxfam, eventually had much greater resources and freedom of action, as did the many other charities with overseas responsibilities. Most established national institutions remained prosperous, whether their activities came within the government's purview or not. Religious institutions with a traditional role in the social services, like the Salvation Army (1865), the Church Army (1883) and many city missions, must have wondered about the efficacy of government legislation, since so many people still fell through the state welfare net. The many institutions not directly associated with personal social services, such as the RSPCA and the National Trust, continued operations with little interruption. The Royal National Lifeboat Institution, whose important operations many thought should be taken over by the state, carried on as before. That lighthouses were run by civil servants and lifeboats by philanthropists suggested the prevailing muddle.

Despite signs that the philanthropic establishment could respond successfully to the new social environment, it was unsettled by the creation of the Welfare State and uncertain about its future in a semi-collectivist society. No longer could it make exaggerated claims about the pre-eminence of voluntarism in British life. To some extent it was the victim of changed public expectations. It was not obvious at the time that government could never fully satisfy them.

In the 1930s, voluntary action was often in the headlines; after 1945 this was not the case, for the war and state assistance had focused press attention on national and material life to such an extent. Local papers tell a different story, for they reported a continuing commitment to voluntary action absent from the metropolitan papers. But at the national level, state spending on the health and social services steadily dwarfed the funds available to charities. Would further government action make the work of voluntary institutions unnecessary or endanger their flow of funds? Would the growing cooperation with government agencies, accentuated by the war, eventually undermine philanthropy's cherished independence?

Opinions varied, and they largely depended on the person's relationship to the voluntary movement. Philanthropists in local causes were less likely to be worried about the future of voluntarism, if they thought about it at all, for they recognized that government was ill suited to take over most of their services. Those in the national societies looked to their endowments and took hope from new institutions like the Nuffield Foundation (1943). Some concluded that the Welfare State was a blessing in disguise, for in freeing philanthropists from former thankless tasks it offered fresh opportunities. This was a view quickly adopted by those in health-related charities.[17] In the House of Lords in 1949, several Liberal peers and Lord Pakenham for Labour took the view that philanthropy would and must endure, for in a 'perpetually moving frontier', it was necessary 'to pioneer ahead of the state'.[18] Clement Attlee, speaking as President of Toynbee Hall, a charity traditionally favoured by socialists, recognized that philanthropy was 'not confined to any one class of the community' and argued that 'we shall always have alongside the great range of public services, the voluntary services which humanize our national life and bring it down from the general to the particular'.[19]

But socialists less sympathetic to voluntarism thought it likely that the days of the independent philanthropic society, free from government assistance, were at an end.[20] In parliament, Aneurin Bevan diplomatically accepted that the Labour government should make full use of the voluntary organizations, but he was no friend to charity. As Minister of Health, he equated it with nurses organizing flag days on their weekends off, which struck him as an indignity in a modern society. Many other Labour politicians, civil servants and students of social policy, transfixed by state social action and their part in its promotion, shared the view that charity was demeaning. As government would attend to everyone's needs from the cradle to the grave, what was the point of it? For those who took this view, Victorian traditions of parochial service and self-help were repugnant, remnants of a tribal past. As Bevan put it, 'a patch-quilt of local paternalisms' is the 'enemy of intelligent planning'.[21]

William Beveridge, remembering his youth at Toynbee Hall, took a more spacious view. In his book *Voluntary Action*, published in 1948, he recognized how deep charitable roots had struck in British culture. In addition to tributes to philanthropic pioneers, including Thomas Bernard for his social surveys, he discussed the role of parish societies, women's voluntary work, children's charities, mutual aid, citizens' advice bureaux and the settlement movement, all of which, though still vigorous, were being pushed into the background in the hubbub surrounding the implementation of government programmes. It was not his intention that the Social Service State, as he called it, which he had shaped, should monopolize initiatives in social action. He wrote to focus attention on philanthropy's rich past but uncertain future and to promote new and inventive cooperation between volunteers and the statutory authorities. Sounding like a Victorian moralist, he detected that strain of social duty in voluntary action without which the assertion of rights was meaningless and without which society could not be civilized. In words reminiscent of Mill, he worried lest too much state control over the nation's affairs outside the home might lead to totalitarianism. 'By contrast, vigour and abundance of Voluntary Action outside the home, individually and in association with other citizens, for bettering one's own life and that of one's fellows, are the distinguishing marks of a free society.'[22]

VI

Conclusion

No nation on earth can lay claim to a richer philanthropic past than Britain. And in few countries is the voluntary impulse so vigorous today. Where it is, as in the United States, it is helped by a lower level of competition from state social provision and easier tax laws. Although the Welfare State has overshadowed the British voluntary sector since the war, it has not altered many of its settled traditions. Today's philanthropists, whether they call themselves voluntarists or believers in 'welfare pluralism', reveal attitudes and concerns long customary. They have shed the narrow religious doctrine and the language of social hierarchy often associated with the nineteenth century, but they are direct descendants of their Victorian forebears in their individualism, with its emphasis on self-help, their moral sensibility and social activism, their belief in progress, and the localism which makes them chary of centralized authority. They are successors of Mill in their political economy, of Wilberforce in their crusading zeal. To some in political life they are the welfare equivalent of the Victorian entrepreneur, efficient and productive.[1] In an age of state supremacy, they make their own choices. In a secular society, they offer scope for the expression of individual values. As ever, they offer opportunities for personal social action outside the home to women and minorities who might otherwise feel unrepresented or removed from the main currents of British life.

A fundamental reason for the resilience of philanthropy is its enduring recognition of the primacy and integrity of the family and the perennial need to defend it from deterioration. The Victorians recognized, though their children often did not, that the home was more than a refuge from the cares of the world; it was the mainspring of identity and self-expression, and in so far as the world outside was illiberal, a refuge of freedom. The state, for all its inventive intervention in family life, is widely seen today as too blunt and impersonal an instrument to provide security for the British family without reinforcements from volunteers. By definition, charity implies a personal relationship, the response of an individual to the misfortune of others. Where it has departed from this assumption it has departed from nineteenth-century ideals. Analyses of the causes of social distress have shifted radically in the past hundred years. Yet the signs are that the Victorian emphasis on bringing out qualities of character which might help people to help themselves is coming back into prominence. Among voluntarists, of course, it has never lost its attractions, for it suits so well the personal services which they provide. As one sympathizer put it in the 1950s, there is 'a strong presumption that the distress of an individual or the collapse of a family circle really *is* due to special individual misfortune or defect of character, and really *does* need an individual approach'.[2]

The tenacity of such assumptions is reflected in the charitable world's present emphasis on family and community revival, which has been given recent impetus by the 'crisis of the inner cities'. A modern report from a Liverpool charity, which would be unexceptional to the Victorians despite the language, sees the root cause of today's social malaise in 'the slow collapse of the family' and calls for the devolution of the 'caring services' to local residents and neighbourhood councils.[3] An article in the *Guardian* argued that 'the health of the body depends on the health of . . . the parish or neighbourhood, with which people can readily identify'.[4] This was written by the chairman of the Institute for Social Inventions; it might have come from a Victorian mother drumming up support for a boot club. Such views, increasingly commonplace, confirm that there is a persistent demand for diverse local charity, in which today's clients may be tomorrow's helpers. Small-scale projects and informal benevolence rarely make the headlines, but they have always been the life blood of philanthropy. They have been obscured in the twentieth century by the shift of public attention to centralized state welfare and the charitable establishment's own tendency to play to a national audience without sufficient regard to its roots in the localities. But as more and more of the national charities, often with the support of local authorities, seek to promote community self-help, perceptions may change.

Both philanthropy and the state have made massive contributions to reducing human misery, but neither has lived up to expectations, if only because expectations have been too high. Now that centralized state welfare is losing its plausibility as a panacea for all of the nation's ills (just as charity once did) perhaps we can take a more balanced view of the contribution philanthropy has made to British life and more fully appreciate its character. Many people regard nineteenth-century philanthropy with distaste, but more often than not their views are based on misconceptions. They dislike charitable motives which operated with little reference to material distress, and forget that religion made sense in a world in which life was so uncertain and its leaving likely to be torment. Modern critics also presuppose alternatives which were not available in the past. To imagine the Welfare State being implemented in Victorian Britain is rather like proposing a British moon landing in the 1930s. It is partly because voluntary work was needed to show and prepare the way for state action that so much was beyond the reach of Victorian government. Critics have been better at describing the ways in which philanthropy paved the way for the state than at doing justice to its contribution to uncovering and understanding the problems it chose to tackle. Thus they have not fully appreciated how fertile philanthropy would remain in a democratic society. Voluntary action did not evaporate in 1948 as many commentators expected. It is perpetually discovering new needs and aspirations.

Philanthropy has always alienated people who seek to improve mankind through a more radical and scientific redistribution of wealth. Inevitably, they undervalue the contribution made by philanthropists in the past to simply coping from day to day with an awesome level of endemic disease, unemployment and other social ills, which were then less well understood. General William Booth, who knew a bit about human misery, said that he had nothing against Utopianism, collectivist or individualist. But 'here in our Shelters last night were a thousand hungry, workless people. . . . It is in the meantime that the people must be fed, that their life's work must be done or left undone for ever.'[5] Here, 'in the meantime', is where philanthropists typically have found their essential work and their greatest rewards. The 'sick child in a fever' uncared for by Beatrice Webb but shouldered by Mrs Browning was and remains their concern. They have always been most effective where they have blended into their surroundings, where their labours are personal, natural and unexceptional, in actions that prevent catastrophe or help people through it, that avert everyday disappointment, or which offer people the possibility of getting outside themselves into wider experience. Various and divided, philanthropy is not suited to move heaven and earth, certainly less so than the state, which is also unlikely to bring forth the Millennium. To evaluate it or dismiss it in the light of any such expectation is wilfully unrealistic. If it makes life in Britain more bearable and human, and gives meaning to the giver in the process, it has success enough.

It has been unfortunate for modern British philanthropy that discussions about it are commonly limited to interpretations of social provision inherited from the state. It is thus easy to lose sight of the variety in the voluntary movement and the moral, religious, and political implications which underlie so many of its causes. Beveridge's liberal belief that 'the distinguishing marks of a free society' were to be found in voluntary action is a useful reminder of philanthropy's other qualities. His remark is not without irony, however, for in the nineteenth century many liberals, who looked at philanthropy from the point of view of the recipients, alleged that it was so powerful as to pose a threat to individual liberty. If these critics were alive today, they would probably be mortified by the ascendancy of the state and might hail philanthropists as champions of freedom. This suggests the obvious: that a persuasive case can be made out for a balance between diverse voluntary initiatives and uniform state assistance in a democratic society. But finding an effective balance agreeable to all parties in the provision of welfare is likely to be as elusive in the future as it has been in the past. In the search for it, we must not lose sight of philanthropy's other meanings, which are so much a part of its distinctive contribution to national well being. For in the diversity and principled rivalry, the love of the *ad hoc* remedy, and the seemingly inefficient muddle that typify voluntary action, the nation has gained immeasurable moral and democratic benefits. These may be the most enduring legacies of those philanthropists of the past, rich or poor, misguided or wise, whose works radiated from the home into the wider world.

Notes

I. Introduction

1 David Owen, *English Philanthropy, 1660–1960* (London, 1964), 527.
2 Douglas E. Ashford, *The Emergence of the Welfare States* (Oxford, 1986), 309.
3 *New Statesman*, 6 March 1987, 11.
4 On this issue see *Privatisation and the Welfare State*, eds. Julian Le Grand and Ray Robinson (London, 1984).
5 *New Statesman*, 6 March 1987, 10.
6 F. J. Gladstone, *Voluntary Action in a Changing World* (London, 1979), 100.
7 *The Times*, 17 Dec. 1984.
8 Neil Gilbert, *Capitalism and the Welfare State: Dilemmas of Social Benevolence* (New Haven and London, 1983), 8.
9 *Independent*, 10 Feb. 1987.
10 Bourdillon, ed., *Voluntary Social Services: Their Place in the Modern State* (London, 1945), 15.
11 Gladstone, *Voluntary Action in a Changing World*, 3.
12 Madeline Kerr, *The People of Ship Street* (London, 1958), 102–3.
13 Mary Morris, *Voluntary Work in the Welfare State* (London, 1969), 257.
14 Parliamentary Papers, Cmd. 8710 (1952), par. 53.
15 Stephen Hatch, *Outside the State: Voluntary Organisations in Three English Towns* (London, 1980), 51.
16 *City of London Truss Society for the Relief of the Ruptured Poor* (London, 1818), 3.
17 *NCVO Information Sheet*, No. 6, Section 2, 1.
18 David Gerard, *Charities in Britain: Conservatism or Change?* (London, 1983), 17.
19 For annual information see Charities Aid Foundation, *Charity Statistics* (Tonbridge, 1977–86).
20 Gerard, *Charities in Britain*, 18.

21 *King Edward's Hospital Fund for London. Annual Report 1986*, 13.
22 *Report of the Charity Commissioners for England and Wales for the Year 1986*, 8.
23 Hatch, *Outside the State*, 130.
24 See, for example, Nicholas Cox, *Bridging the Gap: A History of the Corporation of the Sons of the Clergy over 300 Years, 1655–1978* (Oxford, 1978).
25 Hatch, *Outside the State*, 54.
26 Benedict Nightingale, *Charities* (London, 1973), 308.
27 *The Action Aid Review 1986*, 20.
28 *The Times*, 25 Feb. 1988. See Public Accounts Committee, *Monitoring and Control of Charities in England and Wales*, HMSO, 1988.
29 *Observer*, 9 Nov. 1986.
30 *Ibid.*, 16 Nov. 1986.
31 Quoted *NCVO Information Sheet*, No. 20, 7.
32 See, for example, Public Accounts Committee, *Monitoring and Control of Charities in England and Wales*.

II. Philanthropy ascendant

1 Quoted in Owen, *English Philanthropy*, 89.
2 A Lady, *The Whole Duty of Woman* (Stourbridge, 1815), 23.
3 G. M. Young, *Portrait of an Age. Victorian England* (London, 1977), 25.
4 See F. K. Prochaska, *Women and Philanthropy in Nineteenth-Century England* (Oxford, 1980).
5 Albert Dicey, *Law and Public Opinion in England* (London, 1905), 400.
6 John Stuart Mill, *Principles of Political Economy*, Penguin ed. (1970), 312–13.
7 C. L. Balfour, *The Bible Pattern of a Good Woman* (London, 1867), 36.
8 See, for example, Ellen Ross, 'Survival Networks: Women's Neighbourhood Sharing in London before World War I', *History Workshop* (1983), 4–27.
9 Friedrich Engels, *The Condition of the Working Class in England*, eds. W. O. Henderson and W. H. Chaloner (Stanford, 1958), 102, 140.
10 William Conybeare, *Charity of Poor to Poor* (London, 1908), 6.
11 *Family Budgets: Being the Income and Expenses of Twenty-Eight British Households. 1891–1984* (London, 1896).
12 *King Edward's Hospital Fund for London. Forty-Second Annual Report*, 76. Brian Abel-Smith, *The Hospitals 1800–1948* (London, 1964), 250. For further information on working-class charity and self-help see David G. Green, *Working-Class Patients and the Medical Establishment. Self-Help in Britain from the mid-nineteenth century to 1948* (Aldershot, 1985); Brian Harrison, 'Philanthropy and the Victorians', *Victorian*

Studies, 9 (June, 1966), 353–74; Prochaska, *Women and Philanthropy*, 42–3, passim.

13 *Man's Duty to his Neighbour* (London, 1859), 71.

14 *The Christian Mother's Magazine*, ii (October, 1845), 640.

15 Owen, *English Philanthropy*, 92–3, 105. See also J. R. Poynter, *Society and Pauperism. English Ideas on Poor Relief, 1795–1834* (London, 1969). The most useful introduction to Bernard's ideas remains *The Reports of the Society for Bettering the Conditions and Increasing the Comforts of the Poor*, 5 vols. (London, 1798–1808).

16 E. P. Thompson, *The Making of the English Working Class* (London, 1963), 56–7

17 *Reports of the SBCP*, vol. 5. 18.

18 Owen, *English Philanthropy*, 173.

19 See Anne Digby, *Madness, Morality and Medicine: A Study of the York Retreat, 1796–1914* (Cambridge, 1985); Patrick Joyce, *Patronage and Poverty in Merchant Society. The History of Morden College, Blackheath, 1695 to the Present* (Henley-on-Thames, 1982).

20 E. Evelyn Barron, *The National Benevolent Institution, 1812–1936* (London, 1936), 34.

21 *Essays in Ecclesiastical Biography*, 2 vols. (London, 1849), i, 382.

22 Elizabeth Barrett Browning, *Aurora Leigh* (London, 1857), 349.

III. Parochial service in practice

1 On the visiting movement see Prochaska, *Women and Philanthropy*, chapter iv; Owen, *English Philanthropy*, 138–43; Anne Summers, 'A Home from Home – Women's Philanthropic Work in the Nineteenth Century', *Fit Work for Women*, ed. Sandra Burman (London, 1979), 33–63.

2 A. F. Young and E. T. Ashton, *British Social Work in the Nineteenth Century* (London, 1956), 188.

3 On COS practices see Madeline Rooff, *A Hundred Years of Family Welfare* (London, 1972).

4 *The Devotional Remains of Mrs Cryer* (London, 1854), 43, 63–4.

5 *Dear Miss Nightingale: A Selection of Benjamin Jowett's Letters to Florence Nightingale, 1860–1893*, eds Vincent Quinn and John Prest (Oxford, 1987), 88.

6 Quoted in Margaret B. Simey, *Charitable Effort in Liverpool in the Nineteenth Century* (Liverpool, 1951), 65.

7 On the Ranyard Mission see Prochaska, *Women and Philanthropy*, 126–30.

8 Kathleen Heasman, *Evangelicals in Action* (London, 1962), 37.

9 [E. Ranyard], *London and Ten Years Work in It* (London, 1868), 8–10.

10 C. L. Balfour, *A Sketch of Mrs Ann H. Judson* (London, 1854), 4.

11 [E. Ranyard], *Nurses for the Needy* (London, 1875), 67–8.
12 General William Booth, *In Darkest England and the Way Out* (London, 1890), 191.
13 See F. K. Prochaska, 'Body and Soul: Bible Nurses and the Poor in Victorian London', *Historical Research*, 60 (Oct. 1987), 336–48.
14 Little has been written about the mothers' meeting. See my forthcoming article 'A Mothers' Country: Mothers' Meetings and Family Welfare in Britain, 1850–1950', *History*.
15 Jeffrey Cox, *The English Churches in a Secular Society, Lambeth 1870–1930* (New York and Oxford, 1982), 71.
16 For the annual figures see the *Mothers' Union Handbook and Central Report*.
17 *Biblewomen and Nurses*, vol. ix (May, 1892), 94–5; vol. xiii (Aug. 1896), 156–7.
18 *Charities Digest, 1987* (London, 1987), 156.

IV. Paying the bills

1 Hilda Jennings, *The Private Citizen in Public Social Work* (London, 1930), 18.
2 Prochaska, *Women and Philanthropy*, 27.
3 George Behlmer, *Child Abuse and Moral Reform in England, 1870–1908* (Stanford, 1982), 144.
4 *The First 20 Years' Quarterly Papers of the Church Missionary Society* (London, 1826), xv.
5 Owen, *English Philanthropy*, 469.
6 *Proceedings of the Church Missionary Society for Africa and the East. One Hundred-and-First Year, 1899–1900*, 34.
7 Henry A. Mess and others, *Voluntary Social Services since 1918* (London, 1947), 190.
8 *British Red Cross. Review of 1986*, 2.
9 *Gleanings for the Young*, i (Jan. 1878), 8.
10 Prochaska, *Women and Philanthropy*, 83.
11 *NSPCC Annual Report* (London, 1979), 12, ii.
12 For the above mentioned figures see Prochaska, *Women and Philanthropy*, 231–52.
13 *Ibid.*, chapter ii.
14 Quoted in Archibald Prentice, *History of the Anti-Corn-Law League*. 2 vols. (London, 1853), ii, 339.
15 J. P. Gallagher, *The Price of Charity* (London, 1975), 142.
16 Owen, *English Philanthropy*, 119, 155–6.

V. Challenges and adaptation

1 Brian Harrison, *Peaceable Kingdom: Stability and Change in Modern Britain* (Oxford, 1982), 240. (Essential reading.)

2 Quoted in Margaret Brasnett, *Voluntary Social Action* (London, 1969), 2.
3 *Westminster Review* cxxxv, 1891, 373.
4 Owen, *English Philanthropy*, 525.
5 Quoted in Asa Briggs and Anne Macartney, *Toynbee Hall. The First Hundred Years* (London, 1984), 61.
6 Quoted in Harrison, *Peaceable Kingdom*, 259.
7 *Ibid.*, 258.
8 Mrs Harold Gorst, 'Down in the Abyss', *Sketches of the Salvation Army Social Work* (London, 1906), 87.
9 *Women's Mission*, ed. Angela Burdett-Coutts, (London, 1893), 361–6.
10 *Shaftesbury Society and Ragged School Union. 72nd Annual Report, 1915–1916*, 6.
11 Brasnett, *Voluntary Social Action*, 69–71.
12 Elizabeth Macadam, *The New Philanthropy* (London, 1934), 31, 206. On the role of philanthropy as seen from the perspective of the 1930s, see also Constance Braithwaite, *The Voluntary Citizen* (London, 1938). For a discussion of the relationship between the state and philanthropy in the areas of child welfare, mental health and provision for the blind in the first half of the twentieth century, see Madeline Rooff, *Voluntary Societies and Social Policy*, London, 1957.
13 There is an interesting comparison of the war's impact on Bethnal Green and Burnley in Bourdillon, *Voluntary Social Services*, 235–97.
14 *Shaftesbury Magazine*, xcvii (June, 1945), 11.
15 For further information on this campaign, see King Edward's Hospital Fund for London, A/KE/93, Greater London Record Office.
16 For the citizens' advice movement and other wartime charities see Bourdillon, *Voluntary Social Services* and William Beveridge, *Voluntary Action* (London, 1948).
17 See, for example, John Trevelyan, *Voluntary Service and the State* (London, 1952).
18 This entire debate is most interesting; see 5 *Parliamentary Debates* (Lords), clxiii, 75–135.
19 Quoted in Briggs and Macartney, *Toynbee Hall*, 35–6.
20 See the views of M. Penelope Hall, *The Social Services of Modern England* (London, 1952), 301.
21 Aeurin Bevan, *In Place of Fear* (London, 1952), 79.
22 Beveridge, *Voluntary Action*, 10.

VI. Conclusion

1 On leading Victorian charitable businessmen see Ian Bradley, *Enlightened Entrepreneurs* (London, 1987), and Harrison, *Peaceable Kingdom*, 257.

2 J. L. Stocks, *The Philanthropist in a Changing World* (Liverpool, 1953), 22.
3 *Independent*, 11 April 1987.
4 *Guardian*, 22 April 1987.
5 Booth, *In Darkest England*, 79–80.

Bibliography

Abel-Smith, Brian, *The Hospitals 1800–1948*, London, 1964

Action Aid Review 1986

Ashford, Douglas, E., *The Emergence of the Welfare States*, Oxford, 1986

Bagwell, Philip S., *Outcast London – A Methodist Response: West London Mission 1887–1987*, London, 1987

Barron, E. Evelyn, *The National Benevolent Institution, 1812–1936*, London, 1936

Behlmer, George, *Child Abuse and Moral Reform in England, 1870–1908*, Stanford, 1982

Best, Geoffrey, *Mid-Victorian Britain, 1851–1875*, London, 1975

Bevan, Aneurin, *In Place of Fear*, London, 1952

Beveridge, William, *Voluntary Action*, London, 1948

Booth, Charles, *The Life and Labour of the People in London*, London, 1889–1903

Booth, General William, *In Darkest England and the Way Out*, London, 1890

Bourdillon, A. F. C., ed. *Voluntary Social Services: Their Place in the Modern State*, London, 1945

Bradley, Ian, *The Call to Seriousness*, London, 1976

—, *Enlightened Entrepreneurs*, London, 1987

Braithwaithe, Constance, *The Voluntary Citizen*, London, 1938

Brasnett, Margaret, *Voluntary Social Action*, London, 1969

Briggs, Asa and Macartney, Anne, *Toynbee Hall. The First Hundred Years*, London, 1984

British Red Cross. Review of 1986

Brown, Ford K., *Fathers of the Victorians*, Cambridge, 1961

Burn, W. L., *The Age of Equipoise*, London, 1964

Charities Aid Foundation, Annual Charity Statistics, 1977–1986

Charities Digest, 1987, London, 1987

Charity Commissioners for England and Wales, Annual Reports, 1854–1939, 1950–1987

Checkland, Olive, *Philanthropy in Victorian Scotland: Social Welfare and the Voluntary Principle*, Edinburgh, 1980
Cox, Jeffrey, *The English Churches in a Secular Society. Lambeth 1870–1930*, New York and Oxford, 1982
Cox, Nicholas, *Bridging the Gap: A History of the Corporation of the Sons of the Clergy over 300 Years, 1655-1978*, Oxford, 1978
Dear Miss Nightingale: A Selection of Benjamin Jowett's Letters to Florence Nightingale, 1860–1893, eds. Vincent Quinn and John Prest, Oxford, 1987
Dicey, Albert, *Law and Public Opinion in England*, London, 1905
Digby, Anne, *Madness, Morality and Medicine: A Study of the York Retreat, 1796–1914*, Cambridge, 1985
Donajgrodzki, A. P., ed., *Social Control in Nineteenth Century Britain*, London, 1977
Engels, Friedrich, *The Condition of the Working Class in England*, eds. W. O. Henderson and W. H. Chaloner, Stanford, 1958
Family Budgets: Being the Income and Expenses of Twenty-Eight British Households. 1891–1894, London, 1896
Finlayson, G. B. A. M., *The Seventh Earl of Shaftesbury*, London, 1981
The Future of Voluntary Organisations: Report of the Wolfenden Committee, London, 1978
Gallagher, J. P., *The Price of Charity*, London, 1975
Gerard, David, *Charities in Britain: Conservatism or Change?*, London, 1983
Gilbert, Neil, *Capitalism and the Welfare State: Dilemmas of Social Benevolence*, New Haven and London, 1983
Gladstone, Francis, *Charity, Law and Social Justice*, London, 1982
—, *Voluntary Action in a Changing World*, London, 1979
Gorst, Mrs Harold, 'Down the Abyss', *Sketches of the Salvation Army Social Work*, London, 1906
Gray, B. Kirkman, *A History of English Philanthropy*, London, 1905
Green, David, G., *Working-Class Patients and the Medical Establishment. Self-Help in Britain from the mid-nineteenth century to 1948*, Aldershot, 1985
Hall, Phoebe, *Reforming the Welfare. The Politics of Change in the Personal Social Services*, London, 1976
Hall, M. Penelope, *The Social Services of Modern England*, London, 1952
Harrison, Brian, *Drink and the Victorians*, London, 1971
—, *Peaceable Kingdom: Stability and Change in Modern Britain*, Oxford, 1982
—, 'Philanthropy and the Victorians', *Victorian Studies*, ix, 1966
Hatch, Stephen, *Outside the State: Voluntary Organisations in Three English Towns*, London, 1980
Heasman, Kathleen, *Evangelicals in Action*, London, 1962

Jennings, Hilda, *The Private Citizen in Public Social Work*, London, 1930
Jones, Gareth Stedman, *Outcast London*, London, 1971
Joyce, Patrick, *Patronage and Poverty in Merchant Society. The History of Morden College, Blackheath, 1695 to the Present*, Henley-on-Thames, 1982
Kerr, Madeline, *The People of Ship Street*, London, 1958
King Edward's Hospital Fund for London, Annual Reports, 1897–1987
Lascelles, E. C. P., 'Charity', *Early Victorian England 1830–1865*, ed. G. M. Young, 2 vols., London, 1934
Le Grand, Julian and Robinson, Ray, *Privatisation and the Welfare State*, London, 1984
Macadam, Elizabeth, *The New Philanthropy*, London, 1934
Mackay, Thomas, *The State and Charity*, London, 1898
McCord, Norman, 'The Poor Law and Philanthropy', *The New Poor Law in the Nineteenth Century*, ed. Derek Fraser, London, 1976
Meacham, Standish, *A Life Apart: The English Working Class 1890–1914*, London, 1977
Mearns, A., *The Bitter Cry of Outcast London: An Enquiry into the Condition of the Abject Poor*, London, 1883
Mess, Henry A. and others, *Voluntary Social Services since 1918*, London, 1947
Mill, John Stuart, *Principles of Political Economy*, Harmondsworth, 1970
Morris, Mary, *Voluntary Work in the Welfare State*, London, 1969
Mothers' Union Handbook and Central Report
Mowat, C. L., *The Charity Organisation Society, 1869–1913: Its Ideas and Work*, London, 1961
National Council for Voluntary Organisations, Information Sheets
National Society for the Prevention of Cruelty to Children, Annual Reports
Nightingale, Benedict, *Charities*, London, 1973
Obelkevich, James, *Religion and Rural Society: South Lindsey 1825–1875*, Oxford, 1976
Owen, David, *English Philanthropy, 1660–1960*, London, 1964
Parliamentary Papers. Report of the Committee on the Law and Practice relating to Charitable Trusts, Cmd. 8710, 1952
Pope, Norris, *Dickens and Charity*, London, 1978
Poynter, J. R., *Society and Pauperism. English Ideas on Poor Relief, 1795–1834*, London, 1969
Prentice, Archibald, *History of the Anti-Corn-Law League*, 2 vols., London, 1853
Prochaska, F. K., *Women and Philanthropy in Nineteenth-Century England*, Oxford, 1980

—, 'Body and Soul: Bible Nurses and the Poor in Victorian London', *Historical Research*, 60, Oct., 1987
—, 'A Mother's Country: Mothers' Meetings and Family Welfare in Britain, 1850–1950', forthcoming in *History*
Public Accounts Committee, *Monitoring and Control of Charities in England and Wales*, HMSO, 1988
Report of the Working Party on Social Workers in the Local Authority Health and Welfare Services (Younghusband Report), London, 1959
Reports of the Society for Bettering the Condition and Increasing the Comforts of the Poor, 5 vols., London, 1798–1808
[Ranyard, E.], *London and Ten Years Work in It*, London, 1868
—, *Nurses for the Needy*, London, 1875
Rivett, Geoffrey, *The Development of the London Hospital System 1823–1948*, London, 1986
Roberts, David, *Paternalism in Early Victorian England*, New Brunswick, New Jersey, 1979
Rooff, Madeline, *A Hundred Years of Family Welfare*, London, 1972
—, *Voluntary Societies and Social Policy*, London, 1957
Ross, Ellen, 'Survival Networks: Women's Neighbourhood Sharing in London before World War I', *History Workshop* 1983
Rowntree, B. Seebohm, *Poverty: A Study of Town Life*, London, 1901
Royal Commission on the Poor Laws and Relief of Distress, 1905–9, *Majority and Minority Reports*
Semmel, Bernard, *The Methodist Revolution*, London, 1974
Shaftesbury Magazine
Shaftesbury Society and Ragged School Union, Annual Reports
Simey, Margaret B., *Charitable Effort in Liverpool in the Nineteenth Century*, Liverpool, 1951
Smith, F. B., *Florence Nightingale: reputation and power*, London, 1982
Stocks, J. L., *The Philanthropist in a Changing World*, Liverpool, 1953
Summers, Anne, 'A Home from Home – Women's Philanthropic Work in the Nineteenth Century', *Fit Work for Women*, ed. Sandra Burman, London, 1979
Thompson, E. P., *The Making of the English Working Class*, London, 1963
Trevelyan, John, *Voluntary Service and the State*, London 1952
Vicinus, Martha, *Independent Women. Work and Community for Single Women 1850–1920*, London, 1985
Voluntary Action, 1981–5 (from Oct. 1985 published as part of *New Society*)
Wagner, Gillian, *Barnardo*, London, 1979
Woman's Mission, ed. Angela Burdett-Coutts, London, 1893

Woodroofe, Kathleen, *From Charity to Social Work*, London, 1962
Young, A. F. and E. T. Ashton, *British Social Work in the Nineteenth Century*, London, 1956
Young, G. M., *Portrait of an Age. Victorian England*, London, 1977
Younghusband, Eileen, *Social Work in Britain: 1950–1975*, 2 vols., London, 1978

Index

Action Aid, 15
AIDS, 12
Alexandra Rose Day, 59
Anti-Corn Law League, 14, 66
Anti-Slavery Society, 12
Association of Jewish Refugees in Great Britain, 82
Attlee, Clement, 84
Aurora Leigh, 40, 73

Band Aid, 2, 16
Bands of Hope, 42, 64
Barnardo's, Dr, 16, 64
bazaars, 14, 65–7
Bentham, Jeremy, 32
Bernard, Thomas, 31–4, 43, 55, 85
Bevan, Aneurin, 84–5
Beveridge, William, 19, 73, 85, 89
Beveridge Report, 82
blind, charities, 38, 44
Bombed Sites Producers Association, 81
Booth, Charles, 71
Booth, General William, 79, 88
Bosanquet, Bernard, 70
Bradford, 8
British and Foreign Bible Society (Bible Society), 12, 59, 62–3
British and Foreign School Society, 67
British Goat Society, 17
British Red Cross, 61, 82
Browning, Elizabeth Barrett, 40, 73
'Bundles for Britain', 81
Burdett-Coutts, Angela, Baroness, 60
Butler, Josephine, 73

Cancer Research Campaign, 16
'carers', 10
Carnegie United Kingdom Trust, 77
Chadwick, Edwin, 73
Chalmers, Thomas, 43
Charity Commissioners, 4, 9, 10–12, 15, 17–19, 41
Charity Organisation Society (COS), 25, 35, 45, 56, 70–1, 81, 83
children and charity, 12, 42, 62–4, *see also* Infant welfare
Children's Union, 64
Church Army, 83
Church Missionary Society, 61, 63
Church of England, 57
Church of England Children's Society, 64
Church of England Waifs and Strays Society, 64
Citizens' Advice Bureaux, 82–3
Clapham sect, 32
Conservatism and charity, 2, 5, 7, 17, 21
Cryer, Mary, 46
deaf, charities, 38

district visiting, 43–53, 78
Dorcas meetings, 23, 42

education, 10, 67
Engels, Friedrich, 27–8
entertainments, charitable, 13–14, 47, 55, 62–6
Eton College, 17–18
evangelicalism, 22–5, 29, 32, 37, 46, 57

Family Welfare Association, formerly COS, 83
First World War, 55, 74–8, 80
French Revolution, 21
Fulham Carnival, 14–15
fund-raising, 9, 13–17, 59–68

General Society for Promoting District Visiting, 44
Girl Guides, 75
Gladstone, Catherine, 61
Gothic Revival, 26
Governesses' Benevolent Institution, 64
Greater London Council, 5
Green, J. R., 69
Greville, Charles, 21
Guilds of Help, 29

Harrison, Brian, 72
Help the Aged, 2
Hill, Octavia, 70, 79–80
Hobsbawm, Eric, 2
Holloway, Thomas, 60
Home Office, 3, 73
House of Lords, 84

Imperial Cancer Research Fund, 77
infant welfare, 12, 52–7
Inland Revenue, Charities Division, 17
Institute for Social Inventions, 87
Institution for the Employment of Needlewomen, 64

Jowett, Benjamin, 47

King Edward's Hospital Fund for London (King's Fund), 28, 83
King George's Fund for Sailors, 76
King George's Jubilee Trust, 77

Labour Party, 3
Ladies Sanitary Association, 56
Lancashire Cotton Famine, 28
League of Mercy, 28
League of Pity, 64
liberalism and charity, 24–5, 89
Live Aid, 14
Liverpool, 8, 38, 87
Liverpool Central Relief Society, 70
Liverpool Council of Voluntary Aid, 78
Local Government Board, 76
Loch, Charles, 70, 79–80
London, 28, 39, 43–4, 49–50, 52
  Bermondsey, 38
  Blackheath, 39
  Fulham, 14–15
  Kilburn, 55
  Lambeth, 54
London City Mission, 12, 48, 55, 57
London Hospital, 66
London Marathon, 14
Lord's Day Observance Society, 18
Low, Sampson, 39

Macadam, Elizabeth, 80, 82
Manchester, 34, 66
Manpower Services Commission, 5
Martineau, Harriet, 51
Marxism, 27–8

Mearns, Andrew, 71
Merseyside, 5
Methodist Missionary Society, 63
Methodists, 44, 46
Metropolitan Visiting and Relief Association, 48, 70
Mill, John Stuart, 25, 85, 86
MIND (National Association for Mental Health), 2
Morden College, Blackheath, 39
More, Hannah, 22
mothers' meetings, 42, 52–7, 81
Mothers' Union, 12, 54, 56–7
motives, charitable, 46–7

Nathan Committee, 8
National Art Collections Fund, 77
National Benevolent Institution, 39
National Council for One Parent Families, 76
National Council for Voluntary Organisations, formerly National Council of Social Service, 5, 19, 70, 76, 78–9, 83
National Federation of Women's Institutes, 76, 82
National Health Service, 1, 4, 75
National Society for Promoting the Education of the Poor, 67
National Society for the Prevention of Cruelty to Children, 12, 60, 64
National Trust, 12, 83
National Union of Townswomen's Guilds, 77
'new philanthropy', 80–2
Nightingale, Florence, 47
Nuffield, Foundation, 84
nursing, district, 45, 52, 75

Order of St John of Jerusalem, 82
Owen, Robert, 29, 33
Oxfam, 2, 12, 14, 83

Pakenham, Frank (Earl of Longford), 84
paternalism, 21, 25, 53–4
'payroll giving', 16–17
Peace Society, 36
pensioners' clubs, 8
Pilgrim Trust, 77
playgroups, 8, 12
Poor Law Amendment Act (1834), 35
poor man's lawyer, 42

Ragged School Union, 29, 55, 81
Ranyard, Ellen, 48–50, 52–3, 55
Ranyard Mission, 48–9, 52–3, 55, 63, 65, 75
religion, decline of, 57, 74–6, *see also* evangelicalism
Rowntree, B. Seebohm, 71
Royal British Legion, 76
Royal Commission on the Poor Laws, 71, 78
Royal family, 16, 65, 78
'Royal Knockout', 16
Royal National Lifeboat Institution, 13, 59, 67, 83
Royal Society for the Prevention of Cruelty to Animals, 36, 63–4, 83
Rumford, Count, 32

Salford, 34
Salvation Army, 29, 42, 48, 73, 83
Samaritans, 2, 12
Save the Children, 16, 77
Scargill, Arthur, 16
School for the Indigent Blind, 38
Scout Association, 77
Second World War, 81–2
Shaftesbury, Lord (Ashley), 34
shops, charity, 14, 61
Skinner, Dennis, 16
slave trade, 22
socialism and charity, 1–3, 71–2, 84

Society for Bettering the Condition and Increasing the Comforts of the Poor (SBCP), 31–4, 36
Society for Promoting Christian Knowledge, 35
Society for the Relief of Distress, 70
Society of Friends, 39
Stephen, Sir James, 39
Strangers' Friend Society, 44
Suffragettes, 65

taxation, charitable relief from, 4, 17, 86
Thatcher, Margaret, 65
Thompson, E. P., 32
Tolpuddle Martyrs, 28
Toynbee Hall, 48, 84–5
Truss societies, 8–9

unemployment, 5, 10, 76–9
Unemployment Assistance Board, 78
United States, 4, 16, 19, 77, 81, 86

Varah, Chad, 12
Voluntary Services Unit (Home Office), 3

War on Want, 2
Webb, Beatrice, 71, 73
Welfare State, 1, 4, 19, 34, 83–4, 86, 88
Wellcome Foundation, 77
Wesley, John, 22, 46
West London Hospital, 14
Wilberforce, William, 22, 46, 86
Winter Distress League, 61
Wolfenden Committee, 11
women and philanthropy, 9–10, 12, 23–4, 30, 33, 41–2, 52–8, 62–6, 73–4, 77, 82
Women's (Royal) Voluntary Service, 81–3
Workhouse Visiting Society, 35
working-class philanthropy, 7–8, 27–31, 33, 44, 48, 63
World Wildlife Fund, 12

York Retreat, 39
Young, G. M., 22
Youth Hostels Association, 77
Youth Training Scheme, 6